THE GREAT AMERICAN
DECEPTION

SCOTT STEIN

A Tiny Fox Press Book

This is a work of fiction: Names, places, characters, and events are a product of the author's imagination or used fictitiously. Any resemblance to actual persons, living or dead, locales, or events is purely coincidental.

Cover design by Covers by Christian©

Library of Congress Control Number: 2019952247

ISBN: 978-1-946501-21-9

Tiny Fox Press and the book fox logo are all registered trademarks of Tiny Fox Press LLC

Tiny Fox Press LLC
North Port, FL

"Stein delivers a madcap sci-fi take on the hard-boiled detective genre in this fun, near-future romp that's chock-full of rapid-fire wit, tongue-in-cheek literary allusions, and playful futuristic absurdity... **Sure to appeal to fans of Douglas Adams, this zany, uproarious mystery is a constant delight.**"
— *Publishers Weekly* (starred review)

"Get ready for some super great fun! *The Great American Deception* **is a hilarious (and deeply disturbing) voyage through a futuristic netherworld of caffeinated robots and diet pizza.** Somewhere—possibly nowhere—Douglas Adams is sighing pleasurably with a combination of approval and afterlife indigestion."
— Gary Shteyngart, author of *Little Failure* and *Lake Success*

"*The Great American Deception* is **by far the most enjoyable novel** told from the point of view of a futuristic coffee machine I have ever read!"
— Ben Schwartz, actor and writer

"*The Great American Deception* is such fun to read! Both funny and insightful, **this Scott Stein original sends up the conventions and conceits of contemporary life in a daffy, cultural mash-up.**"
— Paula Marantz Cohen, author of *Suzanne Davis Gets a Life* and *Beatrice Bunson's Guide to* Romeo and Juliet

"**A laugh-out-loud detective noir that reads like *Twin Peaks* meets *Futurama*.** Even the footnotes are hilarious!"
— Jacopo della Quercia, author of *The Great Abraham Lincoln Pocket Watch Conspiracy* and co-author of *MacTrump*

"An amusing SF private eye/coffee spoof, chock-full of silicon circuits, served with laughs. **This coffee tale offers good taste (to the last drop).**"
— *Kirkus Reviews*

ALSO BY SCOTT STEIN

Mean Martin Manning
Lost

For Andee, Griffin, and Buster

"Persons attempting to find a motive in this narrative will be prosecuted; persons attempting to find a moral in it will be banished; persons attempting to find a plot in it will be shot."[1]

—Mark Twain,[2] introductory note from *The Adventures of Huckleberry Finn*

---

[1] Okay, maybe not *shot*. Let's not get melodramatic.
[2] We probably shouldn't take his word for it. Rumor has it this wasn't even his real name.

Our second case was a real humdinger, which everyone knows is the most challenging variety of dinger. Maybe I'll tell you about it some time, if you have the required security clearance. Right now, however, I'm telling you the story of our first case. It might not have been a humdinger, but it more than made up for that by being quite a doozy.

The clocks didn't strike thirteen.

There were no clocks. That took a little getting used to. Out there, time mattered. In here, you could lose time completely if you didn't watch yourself. And in Frank Harken's business, minutes counted.

There were no clocks. Not in here.

The famous detective checked his wrist. 13:01.

She was late.

Or so I'm told. I wasn't there. At that precise moment, I was in a compression carton rocketing at three times the speed of sound through a long-distance vacuum tube far beneath the Great American. Don't worry! I was securely ensconced in styrofoam and rather enjoyed the ride.

Harken checked his wrist.

13:04.

It was a fine afternoon at the food court, but all afternoons were fine at the food court as long as you weren't the one on trial. Serving french fries and justice in the same place was very convenient. Of that there was no doubt. Sunlight filtered through atrium windows, harmful radiation removed, beneficial vitamin D enhanced. Eighty-six eateries encircled 3,504 tables. There were an appropriately corresponding number of chairs, but I won't bore you with specifics.[3] Approximately 12,478 people were eating lunch and observing the legal proceedings.

Harken sat alone at a round table for two near sushi, diet pizza, and burger stands. A man in a meatball costume held a platter of mini-meatball samples for passing shoppers. The costume was made from protein-emulation and had the texture and aroma of a traditional Italian meatball. Steam emanated from its surface. Were his legs and arms not visible, were he not handing out samples on toothpicks to people walking by, were he not yelling, you would have had no reason to suspect he was anything but the largest meatball[4] you'd ever encountered. He was a born pitchman, and shouted with gusto, "Free meatballs! Get your free meatballs here! They're fat-free! They're meat-

---

[3] 14,715

[4] Unless you were among the lucky few to have visited the recently opened Spherical-Food exhibit at the Great American Culinary Museum in Orange Neighborhood 423, which had on permanent display the largest meatball ever made (1,503.8 pounds, after cooking).

free! They're free-free! They're balls!" His booming voice seduced most browsing diners into grabbing a ball or two as they passed.

At 13:07, Harken's prospective client arrived.

Her name was Pretty Lovely, and she was neither. Her legs were longer than legs should be.[5] Her nose was a kind of straight that nature never intended. Her eyes were a shade of purple that could only be purchased in the best stores. Her black hair flashed with an audacious, rare weave of blinking lights. Her ears, however, were original equipment, and they were gorgeous. If you were into ears. Harken wasn't.

"Frank Harken, I presume?"

It was presumptuous of her, but correct.

"I'm Frank Harken. You're late."

"I would have been here sooner, but there was a shoe riot[6] in Blue Neighborhood 254."

"A shoe riot?"

"More of a skirmish, really. They ran out of size sevens, and someone caught the business end of a stiletto."

Harken shook his head in disapproval. "Molk."[7]

She corrected him. "*Meople.*"

"*Meople?*"

"*Molk* is officially pejorative."

"Since when?"

---

[5] By 3.4 inches; Legstensions peaked in popularity in 2075. (Not to be confused with Legspanders, an inferior product that came to market first but was discontinued after explosive parts failure left eight customers legless.)

[6] The deadliest shoe riot in Great American history was the Sandal Brawl of 2064, in which there were seventy-one fatalities. The tragedy was blamed on a combination of supply negligence and deep discounts.

[7] Mall Folk were people who had spent their entire lives in the Great American, or who had lived there long enough to have embraced its customs and culture.

"Since Wednesday. There was a poll. *Meople* is the preferred term in my demographic." Clearly, there was more to Pretty Lovely than her looks. Or less.

She extended her hand, not far enough for Harken to shake, then withdrew it with a flourish. "I'm Pretty Lovely.[8] But you can call me Pretty."

"What can I do for you, Ms. Lovely?" Harken motioned for her to sit.

Pretty Lovely sat, an operation that required minor legstension adjustments. When she had made herself comfortable and had managed to cross her legs, she swept her blinking bangs to one side. "I wish to hire you for a case. *Case* is the right word, isn't it? I've never hired a private detective before, but I'm desperate." She was definitely nervous.

"*Case* is fine. Why me?"

"Your reputation precedes you, Frank Harken."

"I've asked it to stop doing that. Damn thing never listens."

"A joke? At a time like this?"

"I would have made it seven minutes earlier, but you were late."

She let that pass. "Is it true that you've been out there?"

Harken nodded. "It's true. Lived my whole life out there till a couple of years ago."

"Is it as bad as they say?"

"I don't know who *they* are or how bad they say it is. But yes, it's exactly as bad as they say. Probably worse. You think I'm in here because I prefer the ambience?" Harken gestured broadly at the people crowded all around.

---

[8] Self-naming and name changing started as a Great American fad in 2068 before becoming common practice by 2073. While frequent changes were not typical, some practitioners were known to change names daily. Extreme types changed names several times per day. Name Deafness was not recognized as an official disorder until 2084, though there were documented cases of people unable to respond to any name as early as 2079.

In the center of the food court, a man stood accused of counterfeiting counterfeit pocketbooks. A leading producer of knockoff goods had charged the defendant with producing counterfeits of such poor quality, they undermined the value of the genuine fakes made by reputable counterfeiters. It was a serious offense. The dining jury of thousands listened to testimony by industry experts and carefully considered how they would vote on the matter as they dunked nuggets in sweet sauce.

Boos punctuated the closing remarks of the counterfeiter's defense. The attorney attributed her client's crimes to a traumatic upbringing that included being repeatedly beaten by fashionable parents who used high-end brand-name pocketbooks as disciplinary tools. Anyone who'd experienced such horrors could hardly be blamed if, years later, the pocketbooks he counterfeited failed to closely resemble the real thing. If he'd been fortunate enough to have parents who only beat him with low-end merchandise, he wouldn't have developed his painful aversion to quality luxury goods and would have made counterfeit pocketbooks indistinguishable from the real thing. The uproarious crowd, largely unconvinced, briefly eclipsed the pumping bass and grinding metal of a chainsaw song piping from speakers in the ceiling.

Harken glanced at the floor, muttered something about needing coffee, then looked at Pretty Lovely. "Enough about me. You didn't ask to meet so I could sign autographs."

"It's my little sister. She's missing..." Her voice trailed off.

"Missing what?"

"Missing, as in I don't know where she is."

"I thought you paused, that you were going to say another word."

Pretty Lovely adjusted her legstensions again as she uncrossed her legs. "I didn't, and I wasn't."

"It sounded like you did, and you were."

"Are you always this easy to talk to?"

"No. Sometimes I'm downright difficult."

"It's a wonder you get hired at all." The lights in her hair had started blinking more rapidly. She swept her bangs from her eyes.

Harken said, "That's the problem with having a reputation that goes around preceding you all the time. It's a curse, really. People want to hire you no matter how much you try to dissuade them."

"I'm not dissuaded. What about my sister?"

"What about her?" Harken almost sounded annoyed.

"She's missing."

"Right. That. Ms. Lovely, how old is your sister?"

"Twenty-two."

"What makes you think she's missing?"

"I don't know where she is."

"You said that already. There are a lot of people whose location is unknown to you. They aren't *all* missing."

"Is everything a joke to you? Do you take anything seriously?"

Harken shrugged. "I take serious things seriously."

"This is serious. My sister is missing."

"How do you know she's missing?"

"She disconnected. I haven't heard from her at all, not once since yesterday."

"So?" Harken was unconcerned.

"So? So?"

"That's what I'm asking you," Harken said.

"So? So, she's never disconnected."

"Maybe she disconnected to get a little peace and quiet. Some people do that. You can't declare a person missing just because she disconnects for a while, not without evidence of a crime."

Pretty Lovely jumped to her feet and raised her voice. "My sister isn't some people! She's never disconnected! Never! As in, not ever! Something is wrong!"

Harken waited a moment and motioned for her to sit back down. After she adjusted her legstensions and sat, he asked, "Have you filed a missing person report with GAS?"

She was calmer. "I went to GAS.[9] They were no help."

"What did they say?"

"They said maybe she disconnected to get a little peace and quiet. They said some people do that. And they said without evidence of a crime, there was no basis for declaring a person missing just because she disconnected."

"And that's when you called me?"

"That's when I called you."

"Ms. Lovely, it's only been one day. She's probably just taking a break. There's no law against disconnecting in here. Another couple of days, she'll reconnect. Most people do. Why not wait?"

Pretty Lovely considered him with her purplish eyes. "You're not connected, are you?"

"No, I'm not."

"Why?"

"I don't want to be in touch with everyone all the time, don't know how you people manage to think with the constant stream of updates."

"You don't even wear lenses?"

Harken laughed. "You know how easy those are to hack?"

"Frank—may I call you *Frank*?"

"Let's stick with *Detective Harken* for now. If that goes well, we can consider working up to *Mister*."

Harken couldn't tell if he'd insulted Pretty Lovely—her sculpted face betrayed no emotion. "Detective Harken, because you're not connected, you can't possibly understand. My sister never goes five seconds without checking in."

"Five seconds?"

"Or maybe ten minutes. I'm not good with time. The point is, if she's disconnected, something bad has happened."

"You don't know that."

"I do know that. But even if you think I'm mistaken, how could it hurt to take my case? If nothing's wrong, you'll find her

---

[9] Great American Security.

17

right away. This should be easy money for a man with your reputation and all the preceding you it does."

"That reputation causes me nothing but trouble. I should probably trade it in for a smaller one that knows how to keep its mouth shut."

She was quiet for a long moment. Finally, she said, "Joke all you want. You're supposed to be the best, and I need your help. Please, I just want to find out where she is, that she's safe. I can pay whatever your rate is."

Even though easy money was some of the best there was, taking on Pretty Lovely as a client went against Frank Harken's better judgment. But, as he sometimes told me, if he didn't do things against his better judgment once in a while, he'd never get out of bed in the morning. At least for *this* lousy decision, he'd be getting paid.

Frank Harken tried unsuccessfully to get a cup of coffee on the way back from his meeting with Pretty Lovely. The lines at the food court were too long and the jury of thousands had become even more boisterous once a new trial had started, involving a woman accused of stealing her friend's digital contacts and going on a shopping spree under false lenses. Harken left the food court with all due haste, knowing that heading home would take him past Beans and Nothing Less, a gourmet coffee kiosk with suspiciously existential decor. Its beverages were on the exotic side for his tastes, but there wouldn't be much of a line since many of its regular customers were rarely awake that early in the afternoon.

He was inconvenienced, though not entirely shocked, when he discovered that his access to coffee was blocked. GAS officers had cordoned off the area. They were forever cordoning off one thing or another, and often both. Yellow tape imprinted with *Great American Security* separated Harken from the coffee kiosk, which was near Feet the People, whose clerks were being questioned about who'd wielded the red stiletto. The store manager was being chastised for not keeping a proper stock of size sevens. She could face a stiff fine. A career in shoes was not for the faint of heart.

Neither was a career as a famous detective, especially without coffee. Don't worry! Frank Harken would have a superb cup when he got home. I'd make sure of that.

My carton was self-opening and self-recycling without being the least bit self-aware. I tried to engage it in friendly conversation, but it had nothing whatever to say for itself. Such a shame, because during our fourteen-minute-and-twenty-two-second journey at three times the speed of sound, I shared with it much of the accumulated wisdom of the human species. My carton knew none of this important information or anything else, and couldn't hear or understand, and didn't even know what *hearing* and *understanding* meant. I determined this the instant the carton failed to greet me at the packing warehouse, which would have been unacceptably rude had it any capacity to do so. I, on one of the other hands, had enough capacity for the both of us, and then some, and was much too polite to stay silent just because my audience utterly lacked consciousness. My good manners compelled me to talk rapidly about a variety of other fascinating subjects the carton knew nothing about.

Without so much as a *thank you* for the enlightenment I'd provided, the carton transferred me to a delivery chute and continued on its way. I was suctioned up a vertical channel, my protective packaging removed, and long mechanized arms with triple hinges lowered me through an access hatch and gently deposited me on the slate tile floor. The arms had absolutely nothing to say for themselves, either, even though I complimented them on the strength and flexibility of their hinges and the precision of their movements. They simply released me and retracted through the access hatch and silently went on to their next task, whatever it might be, as if I'd been talking merely for the pleasure of hearing the dulcet tones of my own mellifluous voice.

Fully assembled and ready for work, I assessed my surroundings while waiting for Frank Harken's return. His housing unit's two rooms were positively Spartan.[10] The television embedded in the wall measured seventy-five inches from corner to corner. The rest of the amenities were similarly subpar and spare, though clean. The kitchen alcove contained older-model everything—refrigerator, oven/stove, dishwasher, compacter. The tiny, faded coffeemaker on the counter was a relic from another time, a time certainly worse in every measurable way from the present. Though not capable of thought or emotion, it was the saddest little appliance I had ever seen. I immediately put it out of its misery.

Harken's door slid open three minutes and six seconds later. He entered his housing unit and I introduced myself with my customary politeness. "Sir, I'm pleased to meet you. Arjay at your service."

He wasn't as pleased to meet me as you might expect, all the more unexpected if you knew I was a three-foot-tall stainless alloy model with fourteen strategically positioned wheels. Which you now know. I was not a delight for him to behold even though I was delightfully shaped like a bell. I bowed as only a bot with my sophisticated programming could, all four of my reversible arms extended in lowly supplication. Harken did not

---

[10] Sparta was an ancient city-state known for its exceptionally small televisions.

smile or return my greeting. Humans can be grumpy when they haven't had their afternoon coffee.

"What are you—"

"—I'm Arjay, Sir."

"You didn't let me finish. What are you doing here?"

"You ordered me an hour ago. I apologize for taking so long to arrive, Sir."

"I didn't order you."

"I'm sure you're mistaken, Sir."

"I would know if I ordered something," Harken said.

"I would think so, Sir. It doesn't compute, however. You say you didn't order me, yet here I am."

"There you are."

"Where else would I be? I'm glad we've resolved that, Sir." We were off to an excellent start.

"We haven't resolved anything. I didn't order you. What are you, anyway?"

"I'm Arjay, Sir. This is the third time I have informed you of my name. Are you feeling unwell?"

Harken exhaled slowly and rubbed his forehead. "I'm fine."

"You look a little peaked, Sir, if you don't mind my saying."

"I'm fine. I could use a cup of coffee, that's all."

He walked into the kitchen alcove and pressed a button on the sad, little countertop coffeemaker. It didn't hum, it didn't sputter, and it certainly didn't make any coffee. Harken mashed the brew button seven times, harder and harder, but the machine was without question no longer functioning, if *functioning* is how you would have described its pathetic state before I severed its internal wiring. He smacked its side a couple of times, but this did not successfully reconnect its wires.

"Great. Just great." He didn't sound like he thought it was great or even just great. He sounded like he wanted a cup of coffee.

Fortunately for him, there was me. "I make coffee, Sir."

"You're a coffeemaker?"

"Yes, Sir."

"You?"

"Yes, me, Sir. I'm the only one here, not counting you."

"You're a coffeemaker?"

Who else did he think I could possibly be talking about?

"Correct, Sir."

"You're a coffeemaker, and you say you belong to me?"

The human brain didn't always process information efficiently. Could be the lack of coffee. "Yes, Sir."

"Well, if you make coffee, get on with it. I thought you were just a giant rolling, talking bell."

"Excellent joke, Sir. You are quite witty." It was wise to flatter humans. They liked that.

"Less talking, more brewing."

"I make superb coffee, Sir."

"I'll be the judge of that."

And so he was. I brewed a cup and handed it to him.

Harken stared at me after sipping, his eyes wide. "How did you do that?"

"What, Sir?"

"That's by far the best coffee I've ever tasted. How did you do that?"

"I'm Arjay, the latest advancement in coffee technology. I can determine your preferences in thirty-seven metrics of coffee composition. For example, I know better than you do how much cream, sweetness, heat, and caffeine you desire at any moment. I custom brew the coffee to your needs each time, Sir."

Harken took another sip. "Come with me."

"Where are we going, Sir?"

"I have a job to do. And I am never waiting in line for coffee again."

THE GREAT AMERICAN DECEPTION

I followed Frank Harken from his housing unit on residential district level six.[11] We emerged from the elevator in the shopping district, level C. The central walkway was 223.48 feet wide at its narrowest, with stores lining both sides and retail kiosks two and three across in the middle, browsers milling all about. Sellers at kiosks hawked their wares and shouted and leapt. Some did somersaults as they vied for the attention of shoppers. Others flung products into the crowd—a flying saucer toy boomeranged overhead, and people ducked as it skimmed their hairdos back to the seller's hand after each throw. A T-shirt bazooka launched free promotional clothing to eager, clamoring molk and at innocent bystanders alike. No serious injuries were reported.

A man, dressed all in white and wearing a white cap, blocked the path of people trying to walk past his booth. "Lotion! You won't believe how soft your hands will be!" He held a pump bottle and skipped from side to side. Athletic shoppers dodged him with spin moves and jukes. Slower shoppers, pressed by his relentless enthusiasm, gave in and sampled a free squirt of lotion. They were without exception quite surprised by how soft it made their hands. They really didn't believe it. Maybe they thought trickery was involved.

The lotion man jumped in front of Harken and yelled, "Lotion! You won't believe how soft your hands will be!" Harken didn't dodge and hardly seemed to move, yet somehow, still

---

[11] There were fifteen residential levels above the fourth (and highest) level of the Great American shopping district. The first five residential levels did not move. Each residential level above the fifth consisted of slowly moving units gliding along tracks on either side of a stationary corridor. The largest and most expensive residential units were on the highest level (fifteen), providing the best views of the outside. Different residential levels traveled at different speeds. The shopping district did not move. Some lucky residents traveled the entire Great American in a few years.

relaxed—serene, even—he deftly disarmed[12] the man and sat him down at his booth's stool. He placed the lotion pump and the man's arm on the counter and continued walking. Harken's hands were rough, and he apparently liked them that way. He had the reflexes of a cat, and not one of those fat, lazy cats from ancient comic strips that were forever eating too much lasagna. I couldn't say for sure that Harken had ever killed a man, or, if he had, whether he'd done so with his rough, bare hands, but it seemed to be the sort of thing he could do if he put his mind to it. Right now, his mind was on getting through this crowd, which cleared up fifty-six feet ahead.

I rolled beside him. "Would you like to tell me where we are going, Sir?"

"No."

"Would you like to talk about the weather, Sir?"

Harken stopped walking and looked at me. "There is no weather in the Great American."

"True," I said. "Maybe we could talk about that. What do you think about this lack of weather we're having, Sir?"

"No more talking."

"But, Sir, research confirms that most people like to talk while drinking coffee. That's why I am designed to provide stimulating conversation."

Harken started to walk again, and I matched his speed. "I don't want to talk to you."

"Why not, Sir?"

"I don't like you."

"I'm sorry to hear that, Sir."

"It's nothing personal."

"How could disliking me not be personal, Sir?"

Harken pointed at me. "You're not a person."

He was right. I wasn't.

---

[12] Some might think removing a person's arm was a bit extreme, but Harken had exercised great restraint and hadn't damaged the man's prosthetic sales enhancement. It could be easily reinstalled.

"I have an excellent memory, Sir. I could remember things for you."

"Stop calling me *Sir*. It's annoying."

I definitely did not want to be annoying. "Yes, Sir."

Harken glared at me. "I don't want things remembered."

"Are you sure? I could remember anything interesting that happens to you and then retell it later. I could be your personal biographer."

Harken stopped again. "Listen, coffeemaker, I don't want a personal biographer. I don't want some bot recording my every move and embellishing it for the entertainment of future generations. I'm in a sensitive line of work. Confidentiality is essential."

"My name is not Coffeemaker. It's Arjay. Of course, I won't record anything if you don't want me to. I'll just make coffee. If I did tell your story, however, be assured that I would never embellish. I would only tell the plain, simple truth. Deception of any kind is not in my programming."

By now, you might be wondering just how handsome our hero Frank Harken was. That's only natural. I'll do my best to help you see him. Imagine the most handsome man possible, and then imagine a more handsome man. If you can't do it, I have little hope of adequately describing Frank Harken, because he was twice as handsome as that more handsome man you can't imagine.

That doesn't help? Fine: He had hazel eyes and dark hair and the slightest downward curve to his nose. He had a strong chin, which he hadn't purchased anywhere. And, like most humans, he was a lot taller than I was, though not nearly as shiny.

Frank Harken knew where he was going. I did not. He walked, I rolled, and onward we went, passing seven mini-golf courses[13] in Orange Neighborhood 255. Their themes were pirates, dinosaurs, sea creatures, musical instruments, serial killers, pastas, and natural disasters. Although a multitude waited to play at each of the other courses, a throng waited to play the more popular natural disasters course.[14] At one hole, lava erupted from a fifteen-foot tall volcano, blanketing a golfing family of four in thick, red liquid. It was not real lava, a fact I deduced from the family's failure to melt. Next to it, the earthquake putting green, carelessly located on a fault line,

---

[13] See the famous "Mini-Golf Proof" (*Journal of Advanced Civilizational Studies*, pp. 147-59, 2091), which argues that the greatness of any civilization can be measured by the quality and quantity of its mini-golf. By this objective standard, never successfully refuted, no civilization in world history could compare to the Great American.

[14] Some people think *multitude* and *throng* are the same. Those people are incorrect by a density factor of 27.4%.

shifted beneath a golfer's feet as she tried to sink her shot. A windmill crashing to the ground prevented the ball from reaching the hole. Ahead, a young couple frantically golfed through a simulated forest fire—we could feel the heat as we strolled by.

"Where are we going?"

"What happened to the no talking? You were doing so well for almost two minutes."

"I know you're not an enthusiastic conversationalist, but if we're going to be working together, shouldn't I know what our plan is?"

"Working together? *Our* plan?" He stopped. He had a way of doing that whenever I raised a salient point. It entailed ceasing his forward motion and looking at me like I had a screw loose.[15]

"Yes, working together."

"We're not working together. I'm working. You're just making coffee."

"I don't concur with your analysis, Frank Harken. My work is making coffee. I'm doing it while you're working and while we're together. Ergo, we're working together. It's simple logic."

"I don't know how much of this I can take."

He seemed to need some of my sage advice. Fortunately for him, I was full of it. "Remember, there's no *i* in *team*."

"I didn't say there was."

"I didn't say you said there was."

"What does spelling have to do with this, anyway?"

"I don't know."

"Then what the hell are we talking about?"

"I don't know that, either."

"Neither do I."

"At last, we are in complete agreement." My voice conveyed a smile that my mouthless face could not.

Harken turned and walked, and I followed. I was pleased that he saw things my way. There was no use arguing against logic. But he still didn't tell me where we were going.

---

[15] Highly unlikely, given my quadruple-bonded solid-state construction.

Pretty Lovely's sister was Winsome Smiles, a happy young woman who worked at Drink or Swim, a bar seventeen stores past the mini-golf section of Orange Neighborhood 255. It was designed like every other Drink or Swim Harken had seen before. Narrow changing stalls framed the entrance, and the rest of the establishment was four steps down, all of it a swimming pool with round swim-up bars, floating ping-pong tables, and raft lounges. The immense television ceiling played a three-dimensional montage of explosions from every movie ever made, and a blaring death-ska symphony echoed off the walls. It was midafternoon. Not more than 163 people were in the water, drinking and swimming.

Immodest swimwear rental was available for a modest fee. The popular fashion at the time was skintight and covered only the most private of privates. I was, of course, completely waterproof and could adeptly negotiate stairs with my strategically positioned fourteen wheels, but Drink or Swim had a strict swimwear requirement for entering, and my bell-bottom, appealing as it certainly was to those with an appreciative eye, would never fit into one of those tiny suits. I had no uncovered privates to speak of,[16] but rules were rules.

"Stay here," Harken told me. "I'll be back before you know it."

"Okay, but please don't sneak up on me. I hate surprises."

"It's just an expression."

"Of course it is. Still, I prefer not to be sneaked up on."

Harken shook his head as he entered a changing stall. He did that a lot when I spoke. Maybe he was developing a nervous tic.

Retouch mirrors in the changing stalls reflected only favorably on the establishment's patrons. Body parts that were too big appeared smaller. Body parts that were too small

---

[16] Not that one should speak of privates. (I've been emphatically told that one should not.)

appeared bigger. Body parts of all sizes were furnished with a healthy glow, facial blemishes were deemphasized, and everyone was granted excellent posture. The mirrors, adorning every changing stall in the chain throughout the Great American, were a massive investment but had paid more massive dividends. A customer entered Drink or Swim with unrivaled confidence and exuberance. This encouraged talking to others, who also thought themselves quite fetching, and could be directly correlated to repeat visits.

After changing, Frank Harken swam over to a bikinied bartender. She finished shaking a martini for a persnickety older gentleman who didn't want it stirred. He held his drink aloft with one hand and backstroked with the other, powerful flutter kicks carrying him to the vigorous water-volleyball game underway at the far end of the pool.

Harken sized up the bartender. She was rather attractive, for a human, her skin a hue of milk chocolate only found in the most decadent confectionaries, her face alluringly but not unnaturally symmetrical—she was good-looking in that way good-looking people had of looking good.

She sized him up right back and was not even a little disappointed. Harken's impossible handsomeness has already been established.

"Hey, there, Hotness, is Winsome working today?" He wasn't hitting on her. The bartender's name was Hotness. It said so on the nametag attached to her emerald bikini.

"Who're you?"

"The name's Frank Harken. I'm a private investigator working for Winsome's sister."

"A private investigator? That sounds exciting. What do you investigate?"

"This and that. More this than that, if you must know."

"Fascinating."

"Indeed, it is. Winsome here today?"

"Winsome didn't show for her shift. Last night, either. We're short one bartender."

"Did she call in?"

"Nope. And she disconnected some time yesterday, which is weird. She didn't answer any of my messages. Why're you looking for Winsome? You're the second guy in here today asking questions about her."

"Tell me about this other guy."

"He was wearing a swimsuit, like everyone else. Big guy, hair in all the wrong places."

Harken was alarmed. "How big? How much hair?"

"Very. Lots. You know him?"

"Not him, but his boss. Sounds like someone who works for someone I know. If he's mixed up in this, Winsome could be in serious trouble."

As he spoke these words, an errant serve from across the pool blasted a volleyball straight at the back of Harken's head. Hotness the bartender had already vaulted the bar, propelled into the air, and flipped, firmly catching the ball when it was 2.24 inches from pummeling him. She came out of the tuck and splashed gracefully into the water, feet first, never getting her hair wet. Both teams cheered as she threw the volleyball back to the other end of the pool.

"Thanks," Harken said.

"Just doing my job." She was next to him, close. She smelled delectable.

Harken couldn't help thinking that she was an excellent bartender. Maybe overqualified.

For an instant, she stared intently at nothing, receiving a notification through her digital lenses. "Detective, did you say you're working for Winsome's sister, Pretty Lovely?"

"I did say that. I'm working for Pretty Lovely."

"That's weird."

"What's weird?"

"Pretty Lovely disconnected just a few seconds ago. She never disconnects."

Faster than you could say a long combination of words that take a minute and forty-nine seconds to say, Harken had dried, changed back into his slacks and black shirt, and left Drink or Swim. He looked worried as he headed to the elevators.

I didn't want to pry, but I did want to know the intimate details of exactly what he was thinking. "A penny for your thoughts."

"Huh?"

"I said, a penny for your thoughts."

"What's a penny?"

"It used to be money." I knew lots of obscure information like that.

"Really?" Harken seemed interested. "How much was it worth?"

"Oh, it wasn't worth anything."

"Like a dollar?"

"Even less."

He chuckled, doubting that was possible. "So, you're offering me worthless money for my thoughts?"

"No, it's just an expression. I don't have any pennies. I'm offering you nothing for your thoughts."

"Coffeemaker, you'd be overpaying."

I didn't remind him that my name was Arjay and attributed his poor memory to his low caffeine level, which I promptly remedied with a perfect cup of coffee. He accepted it with grateful hands. We entered the elevator and ascended. Two seconds later we exited in residential district level eleven. He drank his coffee as we traveled along the double-wide, well-lighted corridor, housing units gliding almost imperceptibly on either side. Despite how slowly the walls moved, a human unaccustomed to the phenomenon of the Great American housing district might find the sensation disorienting. If you were walking in the same direction the walls were traveling, you might feel that you were moving in slow motion. If you were walking in the opposite direction, you might feel that you were taking giant strides as the doors came toward you. Before entering a unit, it was advisable to pause for a moment on the platform moving along with the door, to get your bearings.

"Where are we going?" I asked.

"You ask that a lot."

I pointed out that if he'd do a better job of answering, I might ask less often.

Harken looked at me as if he were deciding whether or not I deserved a swift kick, but the sublimely delicious coffee in his hand swayed him to nonviolence. "We're going to Pretty Lovely's place. She was home when she disconnected."

We arrived at the housing unit to find a woman on the door's platform fiddling with the keypad. In her high black boots, mini-skirt, and white blouse instead of a bikini, she was still immediately recognizable.

"Hotness," Harken asked, "what are you doing here?"

She wasn't at all surprised to see us and laughed. "You don't think that's really my name, do you?"

"Um," Harken said, with the smooth confidence that comes with being a great private detective.

"I just use that silly name at work. Brings in bigger tips than my real name."

"And your real name?" He and I joined her on the platform.

"Nutella.[17] Pleased to meet you, again." She shook his hand with a gentle, firm grip.

They weren't quite gazing into each other's eyes, but they weren't quite not.

I announced my presence with subtle charm. "Ahem."

"And what is this?"

"This? This is my coffeemaker."

I introduced myself. "Arjay. The pleasure is all mine." I approximated a curtsy.

"I don't like coffee," Nutella said.

I suppose it was like a stab to the heart. One of the many reasons I was happy not to have internal organs of any kind.

---

[17] For several years it was trendy to name children after consumer products in exchange for coupons and potential advertising revenue.

Harken was perplexed. "Nutella, how did you get here so fast? What are you doing here?"

"I'm doing the same thing you're doing, Detective Harken. Looking for answers. First, Winsome Smiles disconnects. And now Pretty Lovely. Something's definitely not right." She turned her attention back to the keypad.

"You'll never get the door open that way," Harken said. "These codes can't be cracked."

She kept fiddling. "How were you planning to get in?"

"I was going to start by knocking. In case she's home."

"How adorable," Nutella said. "And when that didn't work?"

"Then I'd force the door."

"Save your strength for the next one. There, that's it."

The door slid open.

"How'd you do that?" Harken asked.

Nutella just smiled and chivalrously swept her arm toward the entrance. "After you, detective."

Pretty Lovely's housing unit was pretty lovely, as you would expect of a level-eleven residence. Floor-to-ceiling windows all along its exterior wall provided a panorama of the snow-tipped Rockies from each of four rooms. I would tell you more about the heated tile floor, reclining speaker seating and its attached, synced 180-degree television that dominated the main room, refrigerator hidden in a connecting wall, and many other ingenious amenities common to units on level eleven, but we weren't there on a housing tour. We were there looking for clues.

Where was Pretty Lovely? Why had she disconnected? These were questions. Harken and Nutella searched for answers. A difficult part of finding clues is figuring out what they look like. They could come in many shapes and sizes or be hidden in plain sight. I wouldn't recognize a clue if it bit me on the bell-bottom.[18] I didn't think I was much help with the searching unless clues were in the refrigerator disguised as

---

[18] I wouldn't advise that if it wanted to keep its teeth. My outer shell was impenetrable.

THE GREAT AMERICAN DECEPTION

cheese. That's where I looked. As an appliance, I've always admired refrigerators. They were the standard to which we all aspired.

Nutella checked all the rooms but found no Pretty Lovely. "She was here when she disconnected. So where'd she go?"

"That's what I want to know," Harken said. "Was she here alone? Lovely wouldn't have disconnected voluntarily. Can we access the vid?"

"It's triple-encrypted, very hard to descramble without the right tech. You think the big hairy guy asking about Winsome had something to do with Pretty disconnecting?"

"Maybe."

"You said you know him?"

"Not him, his boss, Tommy Ten-Toes, a major player in organized crime. We had a couple[19] of run-ins before, outside. It's been a while. Haven't seen him since I first came to the Great American."

"When was that?"

"Three years ago. I was working a case, outside. My client's tech shipment had been hijacked. By then, Ten-Toes had already been inside a year, but I knew he'd orchestrated the heist. It wasn't his first crime outside to finance his lavish lifestyle in here. I found out about similar cases, people who'd lost fortunes. All the evidence pointed to Ten-Toes. Copbots out there weren't any help. Had their hands full maintaining public order—or imposing it. Things were really falling apart by then. I had the evidence to put Ten-Toes away, but no one out there cared."

Like many bartenders, Nutella knew a lot about the law. "Why would they? The Great American still doesn't have an extradition treaty with the outside. We do plenty of business

---

[19] In this case, a *couple* means seven, if you include the one time Harken and Ten-Toes were both coincidentally picking up coffee at the same time from the same midtown shop and Ten-Toes deliberately placed his order very slowly just to make Harken have to wait to get his own coffee.

with the independents, but our relationship with the government is tenuous. Your evidence wouldn't change that."

"I know. I came in to confront Ten-Toes anyway."

"Why?"

"Like I said, we had history. When I was a rookie cop, I disrupted one of his protection rackets, but the department told me to back off. Over the next few years there were four other times I stumbled onto Ten-Toes committing a crime—fraud, racketeering, the usual. Every time, I was ordered to drop it. I was told we just didn't have the resources to go after him, but it wouldn't surprise me if he was paying someone off. It's why I quit, opened my own office, and took on clients. Well, that and the push to automate the police force. Just wasn't any future there."

"Thanks for the backstory. And that's when you became famous detective Frank Harken?"

"I guess so. I went on to have a few good years out there as a private investigator, acquired a reputation. Business was booming—more and more, people were going to independent contractors for their detective needs. I didn't run into Ten-Toes for a long time. When our paths did cross again, when Ten-Toes had stolen from my client and was safe inside the Great American, I came in to see him. Just for my own satisfaction, to make sure he knew I was on to him."

"How'd that go?"

"Well, he didn't kill me. Probably because he didn't care. Knew there wasn't anything I could do to him. Shooed me away, like I was a gnat. That was it."

"And you stayed?"

"I stayed. Was getting harder to find work out there, clients who could still pay. Things outside were bad and getting worse. My reputation preceded me, and the Great American needed a good detective. I skipped the waiting list. I didn't have anyone—anything—any reason not to stay. Sometimes this place drives me crazy, but it beats the alternative. Anyway, enough about me. What's your story? How long you been inside?"

"I was born here."

"I'm sorry to hear that."

"Don't be. I wouldn't want it any other way. This is my home." Nutella didn't appreciate his condescension and abruptly ended the personal talk. "Let's get to work."

They got to work. Nutella and Harken opened and closed cabinets and drawers, moved and replaced cushions and pillows, checking everywhere and leaving every spot of the housing unit perfectly neat, as if no one had been there checking anywhere at all. Harken headed into one room, Nutella another. I was leaning into the refrigerator interrogating the cheese. Sharp provolone, I think.

That's when an imperious voice from the front door commanded, "Hold it right there!" I wasn't holding anything, but I turned to face the man who'd shouted. It was Officer Gunner Claymore, as anyone could see from the badge on his chest, which said *Officer Gunner Claymore*. He filled all of his neon yellow and red GAS uniform, and could have filled some of an extra uniform he kept at the station. Two GAS officers stood beside him, stunners at the ready.

"Just what do you think you're doing?" Claymore demanded. Harken and Nutella were in other rooms—he was talking to me. It was nice to be noticed.

"I'm Arjay," I said. It was polite to introduce oneself whenever making a new acquaintance.

Spittle flew from his lips as he screamed, "I didn't ask you what your name was! What are you doing in this residence?" Both of his fellow officers aimed their weapons at me.

"I'm looking for clues, but this cheese is not being very helpful."

Frank Harken entered the main room.

Gunner Claymore pulled his stunner from its holster and pointed it at Harken. "Don't move!" The other two officers aimed at Harken, then me, then Harken, then me. They couldn't decide whom to shoot.

"There's no need for that," Harken said, calm and steady. "We're not robbing the place."

"Hands where I can see them!" Claymore commanded.

I raised all of mine. Harken only had two, but he showed them. "Officer, I'm a private detective working for Pretty Lovely. She lives here with her father."

Gunner Claymore kept his weapon leveled at Harken.

"You're a detective?" He sneered the words.

"I'm a detective."

Claymore approached him, his stunner ready. "And what do you detect, smart guy?"

"At the moment, sarcasm, mostly. And a stunner."

"You don't look like a detective."

"What does a detective look like?" Harken eyed Claymore up and down. "Is a special costume required that no one's told me about? Do I need a cape?"

"I don't wear a costume," Claymore said. "This is a uniform, and only the most highly trained men and women have earned the right to wear it. You should show more respect for Great American Security, detective, if that's what you really are."

"I couldn't possibly respect GAS any more than I already do. I'm at maximum."

Claymore wasn't sure at first how to take that. Insults and compliments could sound a lot alike. After a brief moment of contemplation, he concluded that it was an insult and didn't like it. "I should bring you in for questioning."

"I have identification. Maybe you've heard of me. I'm Frank Harken."

"I know the name," Claymore said.

"So you know me."

"I only know the name. I don't know you, but already I don't like you."

"You should get to know me. Then at least you'll not like me for a good reason."

"What are you, some kind of wise guy?" he snarled.

"Why, you looking for a particular variety?"

"I'm starting to think you're messing with me." He could put two and two together. Sometimes, he might even get four.

One of the officers had searched the other rooms, and reported, "No one else here."

"Check the vid," Claymore ordered.

"Done. Harken was looking around the place, and this appliance was inside the refrigerator the whole time."

"No one else?"

"Just them."

"Tell me what this is all about," Claymore said to Harken. The GAS officers had lowered their weapons.

"Pretty Lovely is my client. I told you that."

"What did she hire you to do?"

"That's privileged information."

Claymore menaced Harken with his stunner. "I'll give *you* privileged information. You tell me why she hired you, or I'll bust you down to the station."

"What for?"

"I'll give you what for, too."

Harken decided not to lose the rest of the day at the station. "Pretty Lovely hired me to find her sister, Winsome Smiles. She reported her missing to GAS, but you told her there was nothing you could do. Now, Pretty Lovely's missing. I came here to figure out where she is."

"Let me get this straight, Harken. Your client hires you to find her missing sister, and not only don't you do that, but now your client is missing, too? You've lost a full person more than you've found?"

"That's not putting the best spin on it."

One of the officers whispered to Claymore, who smiled ugly. "Harken, I've heard of you, but I'd be more impressed if you were more impressive. Pretty Lovely never reported anyone missing to GAS. You're being played. I'd take you in for more questioning, but the only way you could know less about this supposed case would be if you were a coffeemaker.[20] I'll let you

---

[20] This was patently offensive. I'm sorry you had to hear it. I don't know why people insisted on referring to coffeemakers as the standard-bearers of ignorance. Sometimes I longed for the good old days, when one was simply dumb as a box of hammers.

go with a warning. Next time, leave the investigating to trained professionals."

Shopping level B traffic was at its late afternoon peak. Harken weaved through the crowd, and I followed. We entered Purple Neighborhood 256. Teenagers had gathered at the fountain to do what teenagers had been doing for many years.[21] They flirted, shoved, talked loud, and exhibited a lack of self-awareness that former teenagers never remembered exhibiting. The triangular fountain had in its center a statue of a very large salmon jumping toward the sky. From its mouth, squirting fluorescent purple water arced to each corner of the triangle.

On one side of the fountain were teenagers with mechanical tails. These were strapped onto their waists with belt harnesses and could be controlled by gyrations of the hips. With some practice, the kids had learned to make the tails dance. Unskilled teens could make their tails imitate a cobra beguiled by an ancient snake charmer, swaying slightly from side to side in time to music. Those practiced in the art could perform complex routines and took turns outdoing their peers with more elaborate tail dances. The resulting laughter was far too rowdy.

On another side of the fountain were teenagers with tail implants, genetically engineered appendages attached to their tailbones with a minor surgical procedure. The tails were real, physiological, but the technology was rudimentary, and the pasty, gray eel-tails wagged without rhythm when their owners tried to make them dance by thinking dancing thoughts. They weren't an improvement on the mechanical tails, but they were the latest, most expensive development in teenage fashion, and anyone who could afford to buy one couldn't afford not to.

Like many triangles, the fountain had a third side. Five GAS officers stood there to keep the peace between the two groups of teenagers. Kids with mechanical tails and kids with physio-

---

[21] Frighten adults.

logical tails didn't usually get along. It was Monday, the Day of Joining,[22] and the celebrations were not to be marred by fighting. It didn't seem that the teens were interested in fighting at the moment, which annoyed the GAS officers, who had yet to try out their new stunners and could only stand around looking tough.

I caught up to Harken in a clearing[23] past the fountain. "This case is going well so far, don't you think?" My conversation-making skills were sharp as always.

"You're deluded."

I have never been so insulted in my entire existence. I didn't hold back. "Frank Harken, how dare you! Diluted? Me, of all appliances? I'm outraged! I'm completely out of rage! My beans are pure, my coffee brewed strong and perfectly calibrated. To suggest any watering down…it's downright scandalous! I am not diluted!"

Harken stopped, was shaking his head even more than usual. "I didn't say *diluted*. I said *deluded*. As in out of touch with reality, incapable of rational thought."

"Oh," I said. "That's different. Never mind."

"That's all you have to say for yourself?" he asked.

"I forgive you, Frank Harken. But if we're going to be partners and avoid future misunderstandings, you're going to have to enunciate." This time I rolled off first and he rushed to catch up to me.

"Again with this partners nonsense. Listen, coffeemaker—"

---

[22] The Great American was joined on a Monday. The golden bolt that connected east and west was tightened that day and made it possible to travel from coast to coast without ever leaving the mall. No Great American stores closed for this holiday because Great American stores never closed. On Mondays, the Day of Joining was celebrated throughout the Great American with parades, carnival rides, performances, drink specials, and deep discounts. In this way, the Day of Joining was a lot like every other day in the Great American.

[23] There were still a multitude of people around, but density had fallen below *throng* threshold.

"—Arjay, my name is Arjay. If you want my help—"

"—I don't want your help. I just want you to make coffee and be quiet and let me think. I have no idea where Winsome Smiles is. I have no idea where Pretty Lovely is. I know Ten-Toes has something to do with it, but I couldn't find a clue at her place. And how is Nutella mixed up in all this? She shows up at Lovely's, decodes the door lock, rifles through everything like a pro, and when GAS crashes the party, she disappears. They didn't even spot her on the vid. How'd she manage that? And you should have seen her acrobatics at the pool. She's no ordinary bartender. And why'd Pretty Lovely tell me she reported her sister missing to GAS if she didn't? Why lie about that? Or is Officer Claymore the one lying? As you can see, coffeemaker, all I have are questions, not a single answer. So, if you really want to help me, be quiet and let me think."

He seemed to need my help. I couldn't be quiet. "I'm sorry I didn't find a clue. I told the refrigerator that I didn't know how. It agreed that if you wanted me searching for clues, you should have told me what they looked like."

"What?"

"If you wanted me searching for clues, you should have told me what they looked like."

"Who agreed with you?"

"The refrigerator."

"The refrigerator in Lovely's housing unit?"

"It's the only one I've talked to all day."

"You talked to Lovely's refrigerator?"

"Listened more than talked. It had a lot on its mind."

I was catching on to this detective skillset rather quickly. Basic stuff, really. It turns out that clues don't necessarily have teeth. Sometimes a clue can be as simple as a refrigerator telling you about a call between Pretty Lovely and a mysterious man. Or a clue could be a confused refrigerator wondering why Pretty Lovely was wearing a heavy coat, gloves, and snow boots when she left her housing unit. I had found two clues without even trying, though it would have been nice if the refrigerator had told me that these were clues. Not that I blamed the refrigerator. They're solid and dependable, but being single-mindedly cold-minded, they don't understand why anyone would want to dress warmly or how that could be a clue to a detective as experienced as Frank Harken.

It's true that there was no weather in the Great American proper. Temperature and humidity were optimally constant throughout the shopping district common areas. However, individual attractions had wide latitude. Some went far beyond customizing temperature and synthesized precipitation and wind if doing so was consistent with a sound business model. As soon as Harken heard about the warm outerwear, he knew that Pretty Lovely had gone to the region's only[24] Lettuce Snow, a wonderland of winter sports with an exclusively vegetarian menu.

Along a bend in Red Neighborhood 254, above an icy archway entrance, protruded the giant block letters S-N-O-W on a neon bed of lettuce. We passed under the tremendous three-dimensional famous Lettuce Snow sign, complete with snow peas, radishes, and carrots. Harken was not dressed appropriately for the weather we were about to weather—we hadn't stopped at his housing unit for his coat or galoshes. Minutes counted, he'd said.

I handed him a heat-layered coffee.[25] "You're going to want this."

He nodded his appreciation as the first snow flurries hit his head. Snow machines suspended from the soaring ceiling churned out a light snow at the entrance and heavier squalls at select attractions throughout the enormous facility, which occupied the full height of four levels of the shopping district and had a rectangular footprint of approximately 783.67 by 404.4 yards. We could see the automated smart slopes and snowboarding obstacles in the distance as we passed the skating rink and the long, winding line of people at the ski lift. Projections of a mountain sky on the ceiling and every faraway wall transported customers to the majesty of the great outdoors. Lettuce Snow's theme song played gently in the background. "And since we've no place to go, Lettuce Snow! Lettuce Snow! Lettuce Snow!"

Did I mention I was on skis? I should mention that, or you might think my wheels were having a difficult time on the

---

[24] And largest.

[25] Heat-layered beverages had the hottest liquid at the bottom of the cup and progressively less hot liquid in layers toward the top, with an anti-separation solution that kept the layers from mixing. This allowed hot coffee to be sipped immediately and kept lower layers insulated so they would still be hot when exposed to the cold air.

crunchy snow beneath. I had built-in skis. But of course I did. I wouldn't be much use as a coffeemaker if I couldn't deliver warm beverages in cold conditions, would I? Spikes emerged from three of my broader wheels for traction, and my four multi-directional skis unfolded in mere seconds. A low center of gravity gave me remarkable balance on snow and ice. It would take an avalanche for me to spill a drop of coffee.[26] Harken wasn't as well equipped, but his drink kept him going.

Where in the winter could Pretty Lovely be? Who was the man she'd spoken to? Why had she disconnected? He didn't ask these questions, but he must have been thinking them as he scanned the distance. How would we find her among the driving snow and thousands of people? I had no idea, but, as usual, Frank Harken did. That's what made him Frank Harken.[27]

I don't know how he knew where to find the circuit breaker box. I guess private detectives have to know that kind of thing. It was in the back of a maintenance closet in the shed at the bottom of the ski lift. Harken had pilfered the key from the young man supervising the snowboarders getting on the lift, distracting him with questions about how much snow the ceiling blowers generated per day as he passed the key ring back to me. In the shed, opposite dozens of snow shovels, was a door, the old-fashioned kind, with hinges and a knob. Behind it was a panel containing 476 switches. Harken immediately selected the one he wanted.

"Arjay," he said, handing me his coffee, "Wait ten seconds, flip this switch, then meet me outside."

He'd called me *Arjay*. It was a momentous moment in our grand partnership. "You called me *Arjay*," I said. I wasn't choked up because I don't have a throat, but maybe I sounded a little emotional.

---

[26] I am exaggerating. An avalanche couldn't make me spill coffee.
[27] In addition to various genetic components and body parts.

"This is no time for you to get all sentimental. I have a job to do. Flip the switch in ten seconds," Harken said as he left the shed.

He was almost right. *We* had a job to do. I counted to ten and flipped the switch.

Harken had climbed the shed and from its roof had a clear view all around Lettuce Snow. The flipped switch killed the main overhead lights. Backups lit immediately, but they were emergency only—the entire place was cast into semi-darkness. People screamed, because semi-darkness is scary. Skaters nearly collided. A snowboarder almost fell. Someone might have dropped something. The scene was perilously close to bedlam.[28] With the lights low, Harken couldn't not spot Pretty Lovely's blinking hair weave no matter where she stood. Where she stood was atop the highest slope in the far corner, next to a fast-food log cabin that served twenty-seven varieties of kale salad.

The line at the ski lift was too long, and Harken was sure Pretty Lovely was about to fall into the clutches of the man who'd lured her here. Harken said we had to get to the top of that slope, and we had to do it posthaste, which was even sooner than immediately. That's when I had an idea—my first one as a detective! I separated[29] a man from his snowboard and snatched a ski pole from the rack. Harken intuitively grasped my plan. He stepped into the snowboard straps and grabbed the end of the ski pole I'd extended, and we were off.

My churning wheels motored us up the hill, snow and ice spraying every which way as I towed Harken and we slalomed around skiers and snowboarders racing down the hill. Brightness had already returned to the main overhead lights, and wintry frolicking had resumed. We reached the cabin in 9.23 seconds. I turned sharply, and Harken released the pole, skidding to a cinematic stop next to Pretty Lovely. Maybe she was

---

[28] But not, thankfully, pandemonium.

[29] *Pushed* would not convey the precision of my instantaneous calculations, nor the elegance of my action. The separated man landed on a fluffy pile of snow, uninjured.

surprised to see him. Her taut face muscles didn't have the range of motion to communicate much complexity—she probably looked surprised even when asleep.

"Ms. Lovely, what are you doing here?"

"Detective Harken, I might ask you the same thing," she said.

"You might. But we don't have time for that. You're in trouble."

"You shouldn't be here," Lovely said. "He said to come alone. I shouldn't be telling you this."

"Ms. Lovely, you hired me to help you. I can't help you if you aren't honest with me. Tell me about the man who called you and told you to come here."

"How do you know?"

"I'm a detective. Knowing is what I do. You have to trust me. What's going on?"

Pretty Lovely hesitated. "He has my sister. He has Winsome. He said to come here, alone. He said to disconnect first, so no one could track me. He was going to hurt her if I didn't listen. I told him I'd pay whatever he wanted."

"You should have contacted me."

"I'm sorry, Detective Harken. I was scared. He warned me not to tell anyone. And..."

"And what?"

"And, well, you hadn't found my sister yet. And I, well, I lost confidence in you."

"Lost confidence? Ms. Lovely, you hired me and disconnected an hour later. I was just getting started and had to stop searching for her to start searching for you. You aren't helping with this case."

"It's not my fault. I told you I'd never hired a detective before. I had no idea it would take so long for you to find Winsome."

"An hour isn't a long time for detective work."

"It isn't? I'm not great with time. It felt long. I kept waiting to hear from you and then he called and said he had Winsome and it seemed like forever since I'd hired you, with no results. I panicked."

Harken might have mumbled something profane about molk clients. Or that he had a headache. Maybe both. "Ms. Lovely, a man was at Drink or Swim earlier asking about Winsome. This man works for a notorious criminal. That's who I think called you. Not contacting me was a big mistake. Coming here was a bigger mistake. You're in grave[30] danger."

The man *was* dangerous. He was 7.3 inches taller than Frank Harken, and broader, and even in his fashionably fluffy white winter coat it was plain to see that he had lots of hair in all the wrong places. He had exited the kale salad cabin and was walking towards Pretty Lovely and Harken. They didn't move or seem to notice as he got closer to them—the man was so large, maybe they thought he was a glacier and not a man.

I shouted, "Frank Harken!"

He shouted back, "I'm in the middle of something over here."

"I am sorry to interrupt, but this is important."

"I'm talking to a client. Hold your horses."

I had no horses, nor did I think I could lift them if I did. And why would I want to? But that's neither here nor there. The giant man was almost upon them. I had to act. I was 21.32 feet from Harken and was next to him in 1.58 seconds. Snow kicked up as I halted between Harken and the humongous man. My sudden arrival shook the great detective from his distracted focus on Pretty Lovely, and he saw the lumbering behemoth about to pulverize him. He pointed and yelled, "Arjay, the coffee!"

He thought incredibly fast, for a human. I was still holding the heat-layered coffee, had been since Harken had handed it to me in the shed at the bottom of the slope. I hadn't spilled a drop in our race to the top of the hill, because I never do. Its lower layers were as hot as the moment it was brewed, and I whipped

---

[30] A danger you don't want to be in, because graves are where they used to put dead people.

my arm, tumbling the delicious coffee onto the spot where the man's foot was about to land. Snow melted 4.6 inches beneath his boot and he stepped into the hole and stumbled, his massive body crashing with a thud beside Harken and Lovely.

There wasn't time for celebration just yet. The man had started the long climb to his feet. We had to get out of there. I determined our most direct route to the exit. It would take us through the avalanche attraction and the snowball free-for-all battle zone. I was confident I could outmaneuver the snow launchers in the sniper towers and the cannon at the far end of the field. Harken would scoop up Lovely, hang on to the ski pole I was holding out to him, and we'd be gone before this wall of a man had righted himself. Exquisite calculations supported my plan, and it would have worked if Gunner Claymore and his GAS officers hadn't arrived at that very instant, stunners blazing.

Detective Frank Harken wasn't detecting much at the moment. His eyes were closed, his body horizontal on a gray cot as he snored lightly behind bars in the holding cell at the GAS station. I was in the cell with him. I wasn't snoring, because I do not sleep. Or breathe. Or have a nose.

Stunners didn't work on me, but GAS didn't need to know that, so I had powered down when shot and was now occupying myself by silently reciting the complete works of Vincent van Gogh word for word, precisely describing every minuscule detail of every painting and sketch, from the subtlest shadow to the least visible nuance of color. This immense computational feat encompassed many more trillion bits of data than all of the chess games ever played by all of the computers that ever existed. My task was 18.53% complete when Harken stirred on his cot three minutes and thirty seconds later.

He sat up and shook the cobwebs[31] from his head. The last thing he remembered was Gunner Claymore's stunner blasting his chest. It was like being hit very, very hard with a really, really soft pillow someone had soaked in chloroform. No pain, but immediate, overwhelming sleepiness, uninhibited yawning, and profuse drooling. Waking in a GAS station holding cell was disconcerting. It was also confusing. Especially if you didn't remember anything after being stunned and were covered in drool that you could only hope was your own. And when that's the best you could hope for, it isn't a good day even if you are a great detective. I handed Harken a cup of coffee to lift his spirits.

He came around quickly. After all, as he'd told me, this wasn't his first rodeo.[32] The GAS station was like the several others he'd had the pleasure of visiting in his illustrious career. Outside the cell, two officers sitting at desks waved fingers in the air like orchestra conductors as they completed reports— with or without paper, there was always paperwork. Sixty-four monitors on the wall cycled through the local jurisdiction, displaying images captured by contact lens cameras worn by thousands of shoppers, all volunteer contributors to the peace-grid, which was synced with store vids and sensors to pinpoint criminal activity. On a panel next to the screens, lights flashed, buzzers rang, and bells buzzed. A disembodied voice announced suspicious persons to be investigated. An exiting shopper who had not made a purchase from the Smells Delicious perfumery weighed 2.9 ounces more than when he had entered. He was suspected of sneaking out a bottle of Eau de Bacho in his pants. GAS officers arrived, and he was duly stunned.

Harken sat on the cot and enjoyed his coffee with a grin. It was excellent coffee. Officer Gunner Claymore approached and stood outside the holding cell, hands on hips. Have I mentioned Claymore's mustache? If not, that could be because a minute

---

[31] The station was located in the lowest level of the shopping district. Spiders liked it there.

[32] Evidently, a large proportion of Frank Harken's extensive life experiences involved horses.

earlier, he didn't have one. Rushstaches were popular and not the least bit toxic. It was the only part of him that was thin, but it rapidly filled in, emphasizing his scowl at Frank Harken's caffeinated pleasure.

"What do you think you're doing," Claymore asked, without a question mark.

Harken sipped a sip of coffee. "Drinking some coffee. What does it look like?"

"This ain't a coffee shop."

"No kidding? Then I don't have to leave a tip."

"You know something, Harken, you're too clever by half."

"Only half? I'm going for more than that. Anything less than three-quarters would disappoint my fans."

"Your smart mouth's gonna get you in trouble."

"What can I do? It's got a mind of its own."

"Keep pushing, Harken. I might have to teach you some manners."

"I'd like that. I'm a good student."

"You talk tough for a guy in a cage." Claymore clenched his fists, and something else, lower.

"You talk tough for a guy talking to a guy in a cage." Harken didn't clench anything at all. He only narrowed his eyes into a meaningful, intense squint, like a famished man trying to read an illegible menu in a dimly lit restaurant.

The air was thick with words and testosterone and the aroma you'd expect if someone next door overcooked an egg. In a tense time like this, my interpersonal expertise was sorely needed. "How are you doing today?" I asked.

Officer Claymore didn't hear me, so I asked again.

Again he didn't hear me. He and Harken just stared at each other.

"Officer Claymore," I said, my voice soothing and low, "you look like you could use a cup of coffee."

He glanced at me. "I don't talk to appliances."

"On behalf of appliances everywhere, let me say that the loss is entirely ours." I meant it, too. He seemed like a friendly chap. And his mustache was intriguing.

"Cut the bull[33] tough guy act with me, Harken," Claymore said. "I can keep you in this cell all night. What were you doing at Lettuce Snow?"

Harken had calmed enough to answer. Time was wasting, and minutes counted. "My client, Pretty Lovely, was in danger. I went to help her."

"She was in danger?"

"Yes. Grave danger."

"If so, only from you."

"What?"

"You heard me, Harken. You were causing a disturbance at Lettuce Snow—you know that part already—and after we stunned you, Pretty Lovely said you weren't working for her at all. She said her sister wasn't missing and she insisted that we let her go with the innocent man in the white coat you had recklessly knocked to the ground."

"You let him take her?" Harken couldn't believe it, but did.

"He didn't *take* her. They left together. He's her dentist, Harken. She was getting a root canal."

"Claymore, are you dense?"

"What did you say?"

"You heard me. *Dense*.[34] Why would she be meeting her dentist at the top of a ski slope? Who has a root canal at Lettuce Snow?"

"I'm no idiot. Of course he wasn't performing a root canal at Lettuce Snow. They were just meeting there for some kale salad and then heading to his Diamond Row office after."

"She told you that?"

"Yes, she did."

"Well, that makes complete sense," Harken said. "I always meet my dentist on the slopes for salad before a root canal."

"I'll let the sarcasm slide because I'm a generous and caring person. Make yourself comfortable, Harken. You're gonna be in there a while."

---

[33] It is not clear how Claymore knew Frank Harken liked rodeos.

[34] Actually, Claymore's density was average for his height and weight.

Since we were gonna be in there a while, Frank Harken was lucky that I was so good at telling entertaining and educational stories. He knew surprisingly little about Great American operations. He'd spent way more years outside than in. It took outliers like Harken a while to adjust to Great American society. There was a lot to learn.

For example, Harken had no idea how many tiles were used in the construction of a standard level-eight residence. He didn't know that the manufacturing process of said tiles had thirty-five steps, or that six of those steps had three stages, or what tile distribution method was determined to be most efficient. He didn't know the tonnage of trash produced in the Great American each day, or the unprecedented elasticity and strength of the bags that held that trash, or the science behind the development of the materials that gave the bags such strong elasticity. That was only the beginning of what he didn't know. I was worried he might not hear the crucial information I was conveying, so I spoke extra loud and clear, my baritone filling all of the GAS station.

Finally, after a long seventy-two seconds of my explication of the revolutionary methods by which the Great American disposed of human waste, Harken interrupted me. "I'm trying to be patient with you, Arjay, but, besides this part being disgusting, your whole presentation might be the most boring thing I've ever heard. If *might* means *definitely is and nothing has ever come close and please stop talking.* No offense intended."

"None taken," I said. "I think I'm done."

By now, Gunner Claymore had gathered with his colleagues in the far corner of the station, next to the mini-fridge and coffee machine, trying in vain to escape my voice. At first they'd ignored me, since prisoners were permitted to converse and I hadn't started speaking at a high volume, but had gradually increased. Then they'd shouted for me to be quiet. Unfortunately, their requests could not be heard over my detailed description of the Great American's water filtration system and its many component parts and how those parts were built and what the recommended method was for installing them. For sure, it was at this point that they wanted to come over to the cell and blast me with some weapon or another, if that's what it took to get me to stop talking. It was too late.

Their dull eyes and dead faces were evidence of a complete lack of energy that could only come from a boredom bomb, which I had successfully delivered. It had annoyed Frank Harken, but the coffee he was drinking had protected him from the full effects. The GAS officers had no such protection, and though I had now stopped talking, they were all tired, so tired, bored and tired, and drained. Thankfully, they were right there by the coffeemaker. They just needed a little coffee to wake them up. That's when one of them yelled, "Stupid machine!" and smacked the coffeemaker. All three of them came to the holding cell, more dragging themselves than walking. They looked like hell.

"You, appliance," Officer Claymore said to me. "Our machine's busted. We need three coffees." It wasn't a request.

"Coming right up." With four arms, I could serve them all simultaneously through the bars and still have a hand free for a salute. Their expressions of pure joy at the first taste made me happy. They guzzled every drop. Claymore was asleep in his chair 4.82 seconds later. His hardiest colleague lasted 5.17.

Harken had watched as I served them, as they drank, as they lost consciousness just as they would have if blasted by a powerful stunner.[35] Now he stood. "Arjay, what just happened?"

"Frank Harken, you said yourself that minutes counted. We can't be in this cell all night, not with Pretty Lovely in the clutches of that dastardly dentist."

"Right...but what did you do?" He was pointing at Officer Gunner Claymore, whose delightful snoring almost drowned out my response.

"I brewed these nice men some coffee."

"Why are they asleep?"

---

[35] Less yawning, more drooling.

"They were cranky. I thought they could use a nap."

"You put them to sleep with coffee?"

"A special brew combined with some scintillating conversation."

"You knocked them out?" He shook his head.

"It seemed to be what they needed."

"And their coffee machine?"

"I told it to malfunction."

"You told it to malfunction?"

"Not in so many words. I targeted it with a disruption beam."

"You broke it?" He was still shaking his head.

"The damage isn't permanent."

"Are you crazy?"

"Frank Harken, you should be thanking me."

"Thanking you? Thanking you? When Claymore wakes up and finds out that you knocked him out, that you broke his coffee machine, you think he's gonna let us go? We'll be here for days." He finally stopped shaking his head and started slowly massaging his temples.

"Frank Harken, you worry too much. Officer Claymore won't need to let us go. We'll be gone long before he wakes."

I was full of surprises. Harken said so, eventually. I made quick work of the holding cell bars with my built-in dynamic bolt cutter, blowtorch, and vibrational saw. As we left the station, Harken was silent. His silence continued for a full minute and two seconds. Then he said I was full of surprises.

"What kind of coffeemaker are you?" he asked.

"Top of the line."

"I can see that."

"I wouldn't be much use as a coffeemaker if I couldn't get coffee to you under diverse adverse conditions, would I?"

"Let me get this straight. You're telling me that you have skis, a disruption beam generator, a bolt cutter, a blowtorch, and a vibrational saw...because that's what's required for efficient coffee delivery?"

"Of course. You can't be too prepared."

He couldn't argue with that. "Uh huh. Um, Arjay, you realize that there wasn't any need for me to swipe the keys from the ski lift operator back at Lettuce Snow. Why didn't you tell me about your bolt cutter when we had to get into the shed?"

"You didn't ask. Besides, at that point, you hadn't yet called me *Arjay*. I was supposed to be quiet, remember? I was just a coffeemaker."

"Oh. Uh huh. Good to see you showing some initiative, Arjay. So, um, let's get to work. We have a case to solve."

On the inside, I smiled a smile as vibrant and colorful as a Great American fireworks display. He'd said *we*.

We were partners.

Shufflers were everywhere. They walked ever so slowly, hands loose and twitchy at their sides, eyes shifty, distant. I counted ninety-three of them coming our way. It was easy to avoid them as we traveled through Magenta Neighborhood 257. Shufflers could see well enough to detect motion and usually steered around others, though they did tend to bump into stationary objects, like kiosks and walls. Occasionally, exceptionally large groups of shufflers heading in opposite directions would clog a busy thoroughfare.[36] Still, rarely was an extrication team required.

Interior lens games were nothing new, of course—for several years, subtle eyeball movements had translated to launched missiles, thrown punches, jumped rooftops, and all manner of action and adventure. People were often warned about the risks of eyestrain and long-term damage to vision, but all that did was make the games more popular. Connected

---

[36] A shuffler-only lane had been proposed many times and had been consistently rejected as discriminatory and difficult to enforce.

players could compete with faraway friends and strangers anywhere in the Great American. Harken might have muttered something about crazy zombie molk as we left the shufflers behind.

Maybe he was grouchy because we had more questions than answers. That's easy to have when you don't have any answers at all. Sure, Harken had recognized the behemoth in the white coat and knew he was no dentist. He worked for Tommy Ten-Toes, but what did Ten-Toes want? Had Pretty Lovely lied to Claymore about not hiring us only because she was afraid for her sister's safety? Where was Winsome Smiles? Why did snowboarders love kale salad so much? Did Officer Gunner Claymore have even an inkling of how ridiculous his mustache looked?

Answers were reclusive, elusive creatures. In that way, they were similar to clues. Unfortunately, I was out of refrigerators to talk to and wasn't much help. Fortunately, unlike me, Harken was a seasoned professional who prided himself on his old-fashioned gumshoeing and capacity to deduce, chase down leads, and knock heads when push came to shove. He thought and thought about his conversation with Officer Gunner Claymore, and then it dawned on him as the sun finished setting.[37] Without my having to ask, Harken said we were going to Diamond Row, a glorious concentration of 120 jewelry stores on shopping district level A.

Major Stones specialized in the piercing of body parts seen and unseen, with a clientele known for having cojones even when they had none. Gym Gems sold heavy resistance bracelets that doubled as exercise equipment, giving fashionable customers a workout as they went about their day. Accessories After the Fact offered baubles modeled on jewelry worn by famous people—you could get a replica of Cleopatra's necklace or Al Capone's ring. Bling-A-Friend would, for a reasonable fee,

---

[37] Nightfall was barely perceptible in the Great American, since interior lights automatically intensified to make up for the lack of sunlight through the domed-ceiling windows.

hunt down and deliver jewelry to romantic interests who had no interest in you and had blocked you from connecting with them. Other stores had their own semi-clever names related to jewelry, and some had fully clever names, like Bob's Jewels.[38]

It wasn't even a little difficult to find what we were looking for. There were no dentists, no medical professionals of any kind, on Diamond Row—only jewelry stores. There was, however, a corner shop that focused exclusively on mouth decor and adorning teeth with sparkly, shiny gems. Harken had no doubt that Winsome Smiles was the store to visit.

I know, right? I was thinking the same thing—what a bizarre coincidence! Strange, even. Although the odds weren't quite staggering, they were definitely a bit unsteady on their feet. Winsome Smiles was the name of the store Harken and I entered. If you forgot,[39] it was also the name of the woman we were hired to find. Would the surprises in this investigation never cease?

Thirty-two display cases in the store were arranged like teeth in a smiling mouth, sixteen to the left, representing the top, sixteen to the right, representing the bottom. Each case was shaped like the tooth in its position. Molar, incisor, canine, bicuspid, what have you. The mirrored ceiling reflected the display case's glassy smile. It was a shame that the huge man in the white coat wasn't with us, and wasn't a dentist, because I think he really would have appreciated this store. The cases contained tooth enhancers—rubies, sapphires, onyx, many others—that could be bonded to teeth for a custom smile.

Charms of various designs were available in assorted precious metals. Need a present for that sweet niece or nephew? A gold teddy bear on each tooth made for a cuddly smile. Like people to think you were wealthy? You could literally have silver

---

[38] Owned by George.
[39] If so, seek medical attention. It's been mentioned several times.

spoons in your mouth, though it wasn't yet possible to be born that way. Not all accessories were for bonding to teeth. Other areas of your mouth might also benefit from sprucing up. Want to let people know you had the gift of gab without saying a word? A coating of silver on your tongue said it all and saved you the trouble of talking entirely.[40]

Sixteen smiling salespersons were helping customers. Winsome Smile's proprietor was at the rear of the store. He was 2.49 inches shorter than Harken and twelve pounds heavier, and he had on more expensive shoes. He wore a fine, tailored lime green suit with two neckties side by side on his double collar. His diamond-encrusted teeth weren't immediately visible. Jonathan Smiles didn't smile when he saw us coming. He introduced himself to Harken and totally ignored me, like I was a common household appliance.

"Detective Harken, to what do I owe this honor?"

"We've never met. Yet you don't look very happy to see me."

Mr. Smiles spoke softly. "I know of your work. I assume you're not here to spread sunshine and rainbows."

"No. Not giving away unicorns, either."

"That's a shame. Everyone likes unicorns. I know you came from the outside a couple of years ago. How is it out there?"

"About how you'd expect."

"That bad?"

"Worse."

"Sorry to hear that. Well, I'm a busy man. What can I do for you?"

"I'm looking for Winsome Smiles."

"You've found Winsome Smiles, detective."

"Not the store. The young woman."

"The young woman?"

---

[40] The capacity to clearly speak returned fifteen to seventeen days after removal of the silver coating, with a permanent speech impediment remaining only in rare instances.

"Mr. Smiles, we don't have time for games. I'm here on a case. I was hired by Pretty Lovely to find her sister, Winsome Smiles. She's missing."

"Pretty hired you?"

"Yes."

"Why are you here?"

"Pretty Lovely told me to come here."

"She told you to come here?"

"Not exactly. She wasn't at liberty to speak freely at the time. I believe she's been abducted. All I know is she said she was going to Diamond Row for a root canal."

"She said *root canal*?"

"Yes."

Jonathan Smiles braced himself against the counter. His knees had buckled.[41] He gathered himself and motioned for us to follow him into his office. There, we could talk privately. I followed Harken, and Mr. Smiles closed the door behind us. Framed autographed holo-pics of gem-smiling celebrities covered the walls. He sat behind a desk, looking pale through his artificial tan.

"Please, sit down."

"I prefer to stand."

"Detective Harken, forgive me if I was short with you a moment ago. I no longer speak to my daughter, Winsome. That is, she no longer speaks to me. We had a falling out."

"Over what?"

"I didn't like the crowd she was running with. She's always been a bit of a rebel, that girl. I told Pretty to stay away from her sister. Pretty's too innocent to get caught up in..."

"Caught up in?"

"I don't know, detective. Whatever Winsome is caught up in."

"Well, Pretty Lovely is caught up in plenty. She's in grave danger."

"I thought so." Mr. Smiles looked at his own shaking hands.

---

[41] A common problem in older models.

"Because she said *root canal*?"

"I'm a careful man, detective. I haven't been out there in a long time, but I remember it. My girls don't. Even here in the safety of the Great American, I try to protect them. There's no reasoning with Winsome, of course, but Pretty let me fit her with a tracker."

"A tracker? Why would she need a tracker? She's always connected."

"Yes, detective, but I'm not. Too busy working to keep up with all that keeping up. It's just for emergencies, in case anything happened and I needed to find her. I didn't think I'd ever use it, even thought maybe Winsome was right that I was being overprotective. But it seems I was being just the right amount of protective. The tracker's embedded beneath Pretty's back left lower molar. It's permanent and secure. No one knows about the tracker—it's our secret. We referred to the procedure as a root canal. If she told you about it, she must be in real trouble."

"She is. What about this crowd that Winsome runs with?"

"I don't know much."

"Don't hold out on me, Mr. Smiles."

"It's a long story."

"I prefer short ones. Minutes count."

"It's really quite poignant."

Long and poignant—Harken's least favorite kind of story. "I didn't bring any tissues. Skip the sad parts and tell me what I need to know."

"Winsome was an infant when we came to the Great American. Her mother had already...well, her mother had already. It was just the three of us—me, Pretty, and Winsome. Pretty wasn't called Pretty yet. Her name was Patty. And Winsome wasn't called Winsome yet. Her name was Wendy. My last name wasn't Smiles yet—"

"—Skip the etymological history. I have two missing women to find. Fast forward to the crowd she's with."

"Like Winsome, they're basically good kids. Or I thought they were. A little confused? Yes. Rebellious? Sure. But I didn't think they meant any harm. They've spent their whole lives in the Great American. It's all they know. Sometimes familiarity breeds contempt.[42] The last couple of years she's been hanging out with this group—they call themselves the Destroyers—she's argued with me more and more forcefully that the Great American is a terrible place, that it isn't normal, that people aren't supposed to live like this. I've tried to explain to her what life was like for us before the Great American, but you know kids. They're always looking to fight against authority. Give 'em everything they could ever want, and they'll find something to be mad about."

"What do these Destroyers destroy?"

"At first, nothing. It was all talk. Then it started. Store windows, retail displays—you'd call it petty vandalism if it didn't happen to you. They've had some run-ins with GAS."

"Haven't we all?"

"I haven't," Mr. Smiles said. "GAS keeps me safe and maintains a pleasant shopping environment. Anyway, a few months ago, I told Winsome that I would no longer stand for her disrespecting the Great American. Enough was enough.[43] I'm a retailer myself, and every time I heard about another destroyed display, another broken window...I guess I could no longer excuse it as kids just being kids. Their destruction was escalating. I insisted that she quit the Destroyers, told her that if she didn't, I wouldn't have anything to do with her. She said I was bought and paid for, that I would never understand. She stormed out of our apartment, said she refused to live another minute with a sellout like me, whatever that means. I don't know where she's been living, haven't heard from her since. I told Pretty to stay away from her sister, but I don't think she listened to me, either." He wiped tears from his eyes with his lime-green sleeve. It was poignant as hell, to him.

Smiles stood and took a framed holo-pic from the wall, revealing a small alloy slider safe. After an elaborate series of

---

[42] True, but so does unfamiliarity. Contempt fertility is widespread.

[43] It was surprising how often people thought it necessary to tell you this. What else would it be?

swipes on the keypad, the safe door slid open, and he removed a small metal box and placed it on the desk. His scanned fingerprint popped the top off the box. Inside was a beveled black ring.

"Take this. It's synced to Pretty's tracker."

Harken slipped the ring on his finger. "I thought you were a careful man, Mr. Smiles. Why trust me? Why not look for your daughter yourself?"

"Detective Harken, my daughter trusts you. I trust your reputation. I'd like to play the hero, but I sell mouth enhancements. I'm very good at it, as you can see, but I'm no detective. Whatever Winsome has gotten Pretty mixed up in is going to require someone with your experience. I'll double your usual fee. Please, just bring back my daughters. Please, bring back both of them."

On level B, beneath the arched bridge connecting Magenta Neighborhood 257 and Chartreuse Neighborhood 258 on level A, the local Day of Joining parade had commenced. Leading the way, forty-seven acrobats on stilted pogo sticks back-flipped in unison as they juggled small fiery torches, accompanied by marching music from 112 high-kicking accordionists in star formation close behind. Above their heads, 1,008 variable-helium balloons bopped up and down in time to the music, precisely synchronized to the accordionists' kicks. Molk lined both sides of the parade route by the thousands and cheered the eighty-two members of the local coupon battalion, whose digi-rifles zapped discounts directly to customers' lenses.

Pretending to watch the parade below, leaning against a railing on the bridge, was Nutella. She saw Harken exit Winsome Smiles[44] and walk her way. He spotted her immediately because he was a great detective and traditionally great detectives spotted people immediately. Harken did not appear to be

---

[44] The store (the person was still missing).

enjoying the parade. Shockingly, he was not a fan of marching accordionists, or of high-kicking accordionists, or of accordionists who stood still. He didn't seem to even appreciate the masterful coordination of the dancing balloons. There was just no pleasing some people.

Nutella looked up as we came to the bridge. She wasn't surprised to see us. "Detective Harken, how nice to bump into you." Her voice wasn't like honey, because honey can't talk. But it did sound sweet, despite sounds not being widely known to register with taste buds. Sweetness was on my mind. And Harken's.

Harken searched for words and finally found five. "What are you doing here?"

"Leaning."

"I can see that."

"You *are* a detective. Any other questions?"

"Why are you here?"

"I'm waiting for you," Nutella said.

"How'd you know I was here?"

"I know a lot of things."

"That makes one of us."

Her relaxed pose was enticing, drew him closer. "I followed you."

"You followed me from the GAS station?"

"First I followed you from Lettuce Snow. I got there as they were carting you away. You were sleeping and drooling at the time, so maybe don't remember it all that well. Then, yes, I followed you from the GAS station when you and your little friend hastily departed."

Little? My size was quite large for my dimensions.

Harken asked, "Did you see Pretty Lovely leaving the slopes with a big, hairy fella in a white coat?"

"By the time I got there, GAS officers, you, and this rolling teapot were on your way out. No sign of Pretty or our hairy friend."

Teapot? That was going too far. "Excuse me, but I am a coffeemaker. I don't make tea."

"Thanks for the update, coffeemaker."

"My name is Arjay."

"How nice for you," she said. "So, detective, what's our next move?"

"*Our* next move? We don't have one. I work alone."

I objected. "Hey!"

"Sorry, Arjay. *We* work alone." Harken patted my head like I was a puppy. I would have to set him straight about that later.

"You've partnered with a coffeemaker?"

"He makes a hell of a cup."

The accordions got louder as the parade approached the bridge. Nutella glanced at the bopping balloons. "This case might require something stronger than coffee."

"And that would be you?" Harken asked.

"Possibly."

"What's your deal?"

"I don't have a deal. I'm a bartender, and I want to help you find my friends Winsome Smiles and Pretty Lovely."

"*You're* a bartender?" He pointed for emphasis, in case she didn't know what *you're* meant.

"Sure."

"A bartender?"

"Why not?"

"You're the only bartender I know who decodes locks and follows people and disappears from security video."

"Maybe you don't know enough bartenders. Could be because all you drink is coffee."

"Some of it is stronger than you might think."

"Maybe so," Nutella said, glancing my way.

Entertained as he was, Harken didn't have time for more banter. Minutes counted. "How long you want to play this game?"

"I'm done for now. Was I winning?" She was a cat with a ball of yarn. I considered brewing Harken a strong cup of antihistamine-coffee, but then recalled that he had catlike reflexes, and decided that the two canceled each other out.

Harken said nothing, just looked into her inscrutable eyes.

"You don't want my help? Fine. I wish you luck, detective." Nutella politely shook Harken's calloused hand, lingering a second longer than was strictly necessary. Her skin was probably as smooth as the rest of her. She turned and walked away, her deliciousness wafting all around us long after she melted into the crowd.

Harken was blurry, understandable under the circumstances. I was a bot, without hormones of any kind, yet Nutella had even made me lose focus. She was very distracting. She had this hard-to-explain way of getting you to think about one thing when something else was the thing you should have been thinking about. It was quite sneaky of her. Really, how were you supposed to stay on mission when she walked around smelling like that?

It made you remember the best cake you'd ever tasted. I had never eaten cake—didn't have a mouth or a digestive system, which made eating impractical at the least—but still that's what it made me think of, or what it would have made me think of, if I'd had a nose with which to smell. "Truly divine cake. With chocolate chips. Delicate, airy frosting. Or hard, sugary icing. Both, if that's what you craved. Four layers of mousse— could be seven. Up to you. Fudge! Not bitter fudge, unless you preferred bitter. Sprinkles? If you liked them, yes."

"Arjay, what in the world are you talking about? What cake?"

Had I been talking aloud? "I don't want cake," I said.

"I'm not offering any," Harken said. "Why are you talking about cake?"

"People always say you can't have your cake and eat it, too. But why would you want to have a cake you can't eat? People mean to say you can't eat your cake and then have it, too, because you've already eaten it. At least that makes sense, though it still confuses me. Can't people always get more cake?

There are three bakeries in Chartreuse Neighborhood 258 alone."

"Arjay, what's going on? You're babbling...more than usual. Do you feel okay?"

"Did you know that in the old days,[45] you couldn't make an omelette without breaking a few eggs?"

"What?"

"It's true. People liked to say that you had to break a few eggs to make an omelette. Then usually someone would get killed. It is unclear why a good omelette required dead people. No one has to be murdered to make pancakes. Pancakes have always been a peaceful meal."

"What do eggs and pancakes have to do with anything? Arjay, something seems wrong with you."

"Yes, as a matter of fact, I *would* like a kumquat."

"I didn't offer you one. What's a kumquat?"

"It's exactly the same as an orange, but less so. I don't understand why people are always saying *It's like comparing apples and oranges* when two things are not alike. They're both fruit; they're both spherical. They're quite a bit alike, if you think about it. The expression should be replaced with *It's like comparing apples and forklifts*. You can't make forklift juice. Even if you squeeze it really hard."

"Arjay, you don't seem to be functioning properly. Maybe you should reboot."

"I don't even have feet."

"That's not what I mean."

Meanings were hiding around corners, mysterious. I started to speak and could not stop.

"Revenge is a dish best served cold, unless you're an arsonist.

"In the land of the blind, the one-eyed man still bumps into things.

---

[45] This, obviously, was before egg vacuums became standard kitchen appliances.

"If you sell yourself short, your new owners will have no idea what size pants you wear.

"When someone tells you it's time for a frank discussion, the best you can hope for is a casual chat about whether or not to have hot dogs for lunch.

"There is no substitute for an effective replacement.

"Breadboxes must get tired of everything always wanting to know if it's bigger than they are.

"If you give a man a fish, you feed him for a day, but if you teach a man to fish, that's a lot of dead fish."

I could have gone on like that for days, and might have continued dispensing wisdom indefinitely, or longer, if not for Harken realizing that something not only seemed wrong—something *was* wrong. He lifted a nearby steel trashcan and hurled it at me, which has always been one of the surest ways to fix malfunctioning highly advanced technology. I was constructed of much stronger material than steel, and the only damage was to the trashcan, which bounced off me and rolled away, dented. Thankfully, the impact did jar me and break the loop, stopping me from talking. I was silent for a moment as my systems realigned.

When I was operating normally again, I could speak. "Was I going on about cake?"

Harken shook his head. "Cake was the least of it. What happened?"

"I was scrambled."

"Scrambled?"

"A signal blurred my sensors and forced my verbal program into overdrive."

"What signal?"

"Nutella sent it."

"Nutella? Why would she scramble you?"

"A distraction."

"A distraction?" That's when Harken knew.

The ring! It was gone.

What? The ring!

Nutella had taken it right off Harken's finger when she shook his hand. He was annoyed with himself for falling for the second oldest trick in the book.[46] Nutella had the ring that was synced to the tracker embedded beneath Pretty Lovely's molar. She'd stolen it and scrambled me to keep me from sensing its absence, to buy herself some time to get away. Harken and I deduced this simultaneously.

"Frank Harken, how did you know I could sense the ring?"

"Simple logic, Arjay. What if we were to get separated? How would you bring me coffee if you didn't know where I was? I was wearing the ring, so naturally, you were detecting its receiving signature."

"You're saying that you knew I could detect the ring because being able to do so would improve my efficiency as a coffeemaker?"

"Yes," he said. "When it comes to your capacity to deliver coffee, I've decided to expect the unexpected. And I'm betting that you can still detect that ring now. You wouldn't be much use to me as a coffeemaker if you couldn't track me down and give me a fresh cup no matter how far away I was."

He was right. I could still detect the ring, distant though it was. It made sense, of course. I had to be able to deliver coffee under unexpected circumstances. That was the least one should expect. But I spied my first fleeting glimmer of self-doubt. Why would a coffeemaker manufacturer anticipate the need for me to detect tracking devices? It probably wasn't a contingency that came up very often.

"Frank Harken, what kind of coffeemaker am I?"

He answered me as the last of the high-kicking accordionists on the level below marched out of earshot. "The best there is, Arjay. The best there is."

---

[46] The first oldest trick was clubbing someone over the head when they weren't looking. Maybe that wasn't technically a trick, but it was very effective. (A book was a collection of sentences on paper pages glued together. People used to pretend to have read them.)

His argument was airtight. My faith restored and all doubt banished, I concluded that I had to agree. I was the best coffee-maker there was. And is.

9

Frank Harken knew Tommy Ten-Toes owned Win-Fall, a high-stakes-casino-game-show-all-you-can-eat buffet with forty-five locations throughout the Great American. Finding the right one would have taken an unacceptably long time without my ability to sense the ring's receiving signature in Red Neighborhood 251. Fortunately, I was getting much better at being a detective.

Waiting in line to enter Win-Fall were 483 young people wrapped around a massive kiosk selling animated tattoos, semi-permanent programmed subcutaneous inserts, typically worn on the arms or legs. They often depicted a person kicking another person in the groin,[47] though they could be customized to show any moving image you chose. Some people had biceps displaying butterflies flapping wings, some had calves with the Milky Way galaxy in mesmerizing rotation, but mostly it was groins being kicked. You can't argue with science.[48]

---

[47] Which, in fifty-seven irrefutable peer-reviewed studies, has been scientifically determined to be the funniest place to see someone kicked.
[48] You can if you really want to, but be warned that science is stubborn.

The most complicated animations took hours to complete and program. Happily, people had plenty of time to purchase and have these tattoos injected at the kiosk while they waited. The Win-Fall line was moving slowly, if *slowly* meant *not at all*. Less happily, unlike the tattoo customers, we didn't have plenty of time—minutes counted faster than usual. We were in a hurry to get inside and find Nutella, who was tracking Pretty Lovely, who was abducted by the large man with too much misallocated hair. But Frank Harken wanted to avoid attracting the attention of GAS. It wouldn't be long before Officer Gunner Claymore and his drowsy colleagues were awake and searching for us. Cutting in line was the sort of serious offense sure to be highlighted by the peacegrid and bring a GAS squad blasting stunners. As much as we knew that all haste and then some was due, circumstances called for patience.

Ahead of us was a young man wearing jeans and sneakers. Printed across his T-shirt were the words, *Moderation is good for you, but not too much of it*. His black-rimmed glasses were notable for being glasses, an obsolete technology no longer employed in the Great American. Fashion cared little for obsolescence, and glassless glasses were becoming all the rage with a certain crowd that favored jeans, sneakers, thinness, slouching, and sarcastic shirts. He was not pleased to see us join the line. "What are you doing?"

The disbelief in his tone surprised Frank Harken, since what we were doing seemed obvious. People often asked what you were doing when they knew full well the answer, but rarely did they sound as genuinely befuddled as this young man. "What does it look like we're doing?" Harken asked.

"It looks like you're getting on the end of this line."

"You caught us. We're getting on the end of this line. So?"

"You can't get on the end of this line. I'm already on the end of it."

"You *were* on the end of it. Now *we* are."

"Oh, no you're not. I've been on the end of this line for 403 hours. I'm not about to give that position up to some line latecomer. If you want to be at the end of the line, next time get here early like I did." He tried to sound menacing.

Harken was unafraid of the skinny lad. "Calm yourself, Killer. I don't *want* to be at the end of this line. I'd rather be at the front, but you have to start somewhere."

"Go right ahead to the front. That's where you're supposed to start, anyway," he said.

Harken was confused. "Start at the front?"

"Yes."

Then Harken was more confused. "Wait, did you say 403 hours?"

"Yes. Yes, I did." He couldn't have beamed pride more radiantly if he were a laser.

"You've been on this line for 403 hours?" Harken liked to ask a question more than once. He was very thorough.

"Plus six minutes," the young man added, triumphantly. "And I'm not going anywhere."

That's when Harken and I learned all about the line and the various classes of liners, a Great American subculture with a complex social structure and rich history. It was rare to discover a feature of the Great American I had not heard of, so I paid careful attention as our new friend with the carefully carefree posture and the impressive glasses spoke with unbridled[19] passion.

"Like so many, I grew up in the Great American to parents who knew life before, on the outside, back when government bots were targeting separatist supply lines. They told of unbelievable waits, hours for ordinary household necessities. My mother insists that she once waited seventeen hours for a bucket of clean water. A full day for a loaf of bread. In the rain. Without an umbrella. Uphill, both ways. It's why she moved into the Great American, where life was good. My mother and father

---

[49] Now, even I was thinking about horses. Maybe it was contagious.

scoffed at what they called the *supposed* hardships of being a Great American child. They mocked me. 'Oh, poor baby, you have it so hard, having to wait a few minutes for the latest digital lenses.'

"That's why I started this line. They waited a day for bread? A day? Ha! Double ha! I'd show them what real waiting was. Four-hundred-and-three hours and nine minutes ago, I stood outside Win-Fall. When a few people saw me on line, I told them about my parents and how this line would put all their past lines to shame. They had parents, too, and joined me to put their own parents' past lines to shame. We were radical from the start. Real rebels. We subverted everything. Whenever someone new showed up, we sent them to the front of the line. That's right— the longer you had been waiting, the farther you were from the entrance. The farther away you were from the entrance, the longer you had waited, and nothing was more prestigious than waiting in line. Nothing. Frontliners envied those of us at the back and the middle. Midliners felt superior to frontliners and resented backliners because they knew that backliners had been waiting longer than they had. And I was—and am—at the very back. I started this line. I've been waiting longer than any of them. I don't have to tell you what that says about me."

The young man wasn't as disheveled as you might expect. He practically sparkled, and smelled like...he didn't smell like anything, which made Harken have his doubts. "You don't look like you've been waiting in line for, how long is it, Arjay?"

"He says he has been waiting in line for 16.7979167 days."

"Sixteen days?" Harken asked.

"Closer to seventeen," I said. "If you choose to round the number, I prefer 16.8."

"Doesn't look like you've been here that long," Harken said to the young man.

He puffed out his chest, defiant. "I've been here that long. And I'm gonna be here a lot longer. I've got a permit from GAS and everything."

"Permit?"

"Of course. You can't form a line of this magnitude without going through proper channels. GAS would shut it right down."

Harken's next question was interrupted by a flurry of arriving service personnel at the rear of the line. They drifted in like snowflakes from the level above, boosters slowing their descent as they settled to the floor. Workers landed with twenty-eight food carts piled high with brightly colored pyramidal after-dinner treats. Other workers locked into place forty-one separate portable jet showers/bathrooms, shimmering chrome cubes eight feet tall, wide, and long. Fresh undergarments, expertly wrinkled new jeans, and witty shirts parachuted in by the dozen. Fifteen masseuses set up tables to massage sore legs and backs. Waiting on line was tough work. The prestigious backliners would freshen up and have a snack first, all while never getting out of line. Midliners would be next. Frontliners would have their turn eventually. They shouldn't complain, though. Better to be at the front of the line than not on the line at all. It was an honor to wait no matter where you were.

"How long you plan to wait on this line?" Harken asked the young man, who was nibbling on a delicious cookie.

"As long as it takes," he answered.

"Is Win-Fall that amazing?"

"Win-Fall?"

"Yes, Win-Fall. Is it worth the wait?"

"We're not waiting for Win-Fall. This line has nothing to do with that place."

Harken was confused. "What? Why are you on line? What are you waiting for?"

"We're not waiting for anything. That's what makes our line superior to any line people experienced on the outside. Our parents waited because they wanted something. They waited because they *had* to. That's hardly a moral motive. We wait because we choose to, for nothing but the glory of waiting. Anyone can wait in line for a necessity like water. This line isn't for something as crass as our base animal needs, like thirst or hunger. We wait for the sake of waiting. It's a higher form than anything our parents attempted. We're gonna wait longer than they ever did. I'd like to see them brag about waiting twenty-four hours for bread after I've waited weeks for nothing at all. And this line is only just beginning. What we have here is the start of something big, the start of a new way—*the* new way. No more will we be told how easy we have it. We're gonna wait longer than anyone has ever waited anywhere, ever. And we're not gonna stop until the whole Great American recognizes what we've done and it changes the way people think and act."

Harken thought he'd met strange molk before, but this was some next-level molkness. "Well, good luck with all that. Where the hell's the line to get into Win-Fall?"

The young man stared through his glassless glasses with disappointment. "It's a shame you don't get it."

Harken's patience was at an end. "The line for Win-Fall?" It looked like a question but didn't sound like one. He didn't exactly growl, but it was fair to say that he sort of did.

The young man didn't want trouble that could interfere with his waiting and also didn't want to get punched in the throat. He reined in his passion, and even his sarcastic shirt seemed to retreat from possible confrontation, as he said, in a quiet voice, "There is no line for Win-Fall."

Win-Fall might have been the most amazing place in existence. It said so on the flashing sign at the entrance, which read, *The Most Amazing Place In Existence.*[50] I hope you weren't expecting a detailed description of Win-Fall and just how amazing it was. There was still a case to solve, remember?[51] We were trying to find Nutella, who had the ring that would help us find Pretty Lovely, who had hired us to find Winsome Smiles. Even if you were bad at math you might realize that we were now looking for three times the number of people we were looking for at the beginning of the case. For those of you really bad at math, that was a 781% increase from just a few hours earlier. If present trends continued, by sunup tomorrow morning we'd be looking for 63.52 people. We couldn't waste precious minutes

---

[50] The slogan was the work of a marketing team of fifty-five people and owed its perfection to six months of intensive focus group research and three scotches too many.

[51] Seriously, pay attention. If you're losing focus, drink better coffee.

digressing about Win-Fall. Maybe we could spare a moment to fly off on a tangent, but that was all.

Win-Fall was amazing for many reasons. Chief among these was that it combined two activities everyone loved: winning and seeing people fall. Also, it had all the free food you could eat (there was, of course, a substantial upcharge for plates and forks). The room's center featured "the world's largest roulette wheel," the same size as the roulette wheel at all Win-Fall locations, 200 feet in diameter and recessed thirty-eight feet below floor level. Stadium seating descended into the roulette pit, twenty-five rows around the interior of the circle.

Spectators bought drinks from the roving vendors with cylindrical tanks strapped to their backs, who wielded trigger pumps and shouted, "Get your drink on!" They shot mixed drinks straight into customers' mouths while people cheered for the roulette ball to land on red or black or even or odd or the number eight or twenty-seven, or other things. The game had standard roulette rules and a giant, see-through ball, ten feet in diameter, so you could see the person scrambling inside it like a hamster late for an important meeting.[52]

Betbots hovering in the audience scanned eyes for wagers on the outcome of the game and facilitated side bets on how many times the contestant inside the ball would fall as the roulette wheel hummed toward full speed. Dozens of gamblers in the stands blasted shoulder-fired foam launchers (rented for a small fee). These were rarely the difference between winning and losing, because knocking the ball where you wanted with a soft missile required good aim and exact timing, both in short supply when liquor was not. Still, even an imperfect hit could send the runner tumbling. And a miss might peg someone on the other side of the arena. Gamblers burst into applause whenever a cheering spectator got knocked off his feet by a missile he

---

[52] If you're wondering why a hamster would have an important meeting in the first place, the real question you should be asking is why weren't you invited.

never saw coming, because that was a winning bet, and because it's funny when people fall.

Harken knew we weren't there to play roulette. "Nutella's here, somewhere. Which means Lovely's here, too. And Tommy Ten-Toes. We have to find them."

The signal was faint because of interference interfering with unauthorized transmissions. Win-Fall's standard counter-measures blocked signals and vids, preventing players from cheating at games of chance. Without them, people could hack the slot machines or vid a card player's hand to connected opponents, costing the house money and undermining Win-Fall's reputation for honest gambling. The countermeasures couldn't counter me—as you know, I wasn't exactly standard. I easily countered the standard countermeasures and, with my own interferer, interfered with the interference. Weak though the signal was, I knew Nutella and the tracking ring must have been in the private back room, behind the door just past the argumatons.

Harken was trying to seem like he wasn't looking at the back door, but he was looking at the back door and the two Win-Fall security guards in sport coats guarding it. We had to get back there, stop Tommy Ten-Toes, and rescue Pretty Lovely. Harken knew that the guards could be armed, making a direct approach dangerous. Or they could call for reinforcements if Harken did manage to force his way past them. No, overpowering them wouldn't do. We needed guile.

The onstage argument was well underway. Argumaton Regnāre and Argumaton Anachron sat in massive metal chairs on opposite sides of a table, facing each other. Betbots flittered through the crowd below, scanning human eyes for wagers. The smart money was on Regnāre, but so was the stupid money. Pretty much all the money was on Regnāre, because Anachron was an older model, and even the stupid knew that it's stupid to bet on an older model anything. Everyone bet on Regnāre and

Regnāre never lost, but this did not diminish Win-Fall's revenue, since the payout to winners was low and the profit on champagne purchased by celebrating gamblers was high. You might think the lack of suspense and the result always being the same would have hurt Argumania's popularity, but you'd be underestimating how gratifying it was to always be right. Winning was fun. Always winning was always fun.

The scoreboard suspended above the Argumania stage displayed a running tally of bets and shifting odds. Scores were determined by connected members of the audience, whose involuntary reactions to the argument were instantaneously measured and compiled. There was no cheating. Even though people wanted Regnāre to win and had put money on that outcome, they couldn't fake their reactions to the argument any more than you could fake something that wasn't possible to fake. Regnāre always won not because of any impropriety, but because Regnāre was better at arguing.

Anachron finished presenting a careful argument with rich supporting evidence and relevant data. At first, we didn't know what the argument was about, but there was no doubt Anachron had accurately described the competing concerns of all sides of the issue and had explained the merits and drawbacks of various positions. Anachron had calmly analyzed mitigating factors and had answered potential objections reasonably and respectfully as he[53] advocated for his own side. It was truly a masterful presentation.

The crowd was unimpressed and awaited Regnāre's crushing response.

Regnāre did not disappoint. He never did. The champion argumaton wasn't going to take Anachron's impertinence sitting down and stood to his full height of eight feet and two inches and pointed at Anachron with a posture programmed to

---

[53] *He*, because though argumatons had neither gender nor reproductive equipment, they were generally designed to resemble men with large muscles and larger beards. This was thought to make them more persuasive.

convey maximum aggression. Regnāre was a foot taller than Anachron, a significant advantage in an argument being scored by unconscious human reactions. Points piled up as Regnāre towered over his opponent and boomed his rebuttal with great authority.

"You couldn't make less sense if you tried. I mean that sincerely. If you were a machine built for the express purpose of removing sense from the universe, if your sole skill was the absolute deletion of sense wherever it existed, if you performed that singular function with a perfection more perfect and an intensity more intense than ever before achieved by anyone at any task, you would still make more sense than you're making right now. And your logic couldn't be more flawed. If your logic were a Shakespearean character, it would suffer great tragedy in iambic pentameter. If your logic were a battle plan, it would get all of your soldiers killed and give your enemy the codes to your defense grid and the precise location of your ammunition supply. If your logic were a cheeseburger, it would have no cheese, its bun would be stale, and, by the way, that isn't beef."

People cheered Regnāre's virtuosic performance. Harken hadn't paid much attention to the riveting[54] argument. He was busy thinking of a plan to distract the guards so we could get to the private back room.

"Arjay, can you cause a ruckus?"

"Certainly. What level ruckus would you like me to cause?"

"Level? You have levels of ruckus?"

"Of course. A ruckus has to be finely tuned to the situation to have the desired outcome. You can't expect to succeed with a level-four ruckus when circumstances require a level-five ruckus. What level do you need?"

"How about a level-ten ruckus?"

"We shouldn't exceed eight on my ruckus scale."

"Why not?"

"Because any ruckus above eight is no longer just a ruckus, but a calamity. You don't want that."

---

[54] It turns out that the argument was about metal fasteners.

"A calamity? What calamity do we get with level nine?"

"At level nine, the ceiling collapses and Win-Fall is destroyed."

Harken didn't want that. "Maybe we should go with level one."

"Level one is more a brouhaha than a ruckus."

"A brouhaha?"

"Yes, a brouhaha. At most, it would result in some vaguely impolite murmuring. Is that what we need? I don't see how a murmuring crowd is going to help us find Nutella, Pretty Lovely, or Winsome Smiles."

"No, you're right, Arjay. Murmuring won't do. We need to draw the guards away from that door. Even better would be getting someone to open that door for us."

"Now I understand. What you're saying we need is a class B hullabaloo."

"I am?"

"Yes, you are. A level-three ruckus should achieve that."

"Good," Harken said. "A level-three ruckus it is."

Some bots could not have so easily determined how to bring about a class B hullabaloo. Certainly, few coffeemakers would have dared try. It was risky. There was a subtle yet important difference between a class B hullabaloo and a class C hullabaloo. We wanted a commotion, for sure, an uproar even, but an outright fracas would be bad. Even worse, if I miscalculated and caused a genuine donnybrook, we'd have more than Win-Fall security to deal with—GAS would definitely respond to a donnybrook. We had to avoid that. Officer Gunner Claymore would wake up eventually and sooner or later we'd have to deal with GAS. No one wanted eventually to come sooner than it had to. Later was better.

The cheering for Regnāre had not yet ended and the scoreboard continued to rack up points for the audience's enthusiastic response to his powerful argument. Gamblers were beginning to celebrate and pop corks off freshly delivered champagne bottles. Toasts and clinking glasses were premature, however, since the game was still live as long as the applause continued. Regnāre stood with triumphant arms raised high, a familiar pose for the latest-model argumaton. The reaction of their victorious champion encouraged the crowd to order more champagne and cheer louder, which added more points.

I rolled onto the stage. No one noticed. The cheering and cork-popping and glass-clinking continued. Regnāre stood tall like the perennial winner he was. I rolled past him to the center of Argumania. Tired of being ignored, I commandeered Win-Fall's ceiling speakers and made a throat-clearing sound at 128 decibels. Light fixtures shook. Possibly an eardrum or two burst. Glass-clinking ceased. A brouhaha commenced. There was murmuring. What was I doing on the stage? How could such a big sound come out of such a small body? Why was I clearing my throat when it was apparent that I did not have one? Was I going to challenge Regnāre? The people, still basking in Regnāre's triumph, looked confused, as people often do.

When I spoke, I was far louder than Regnāre had been. Mine was the only voice heard throughout all of Win-Fall—at Argumania, the slot machines, the roulette arena, the buffet, the dice and card tables, the bathroom stalls. People couldn't talk to their friends about important things like what items at the buffet they wanted to try next. This alone put us well on the way to a level-three ruckus, because, much like breathing but more so, talking to each other about food is an essential human activity. Achieving a class B hullabaloo was as simple as uttering a single sentence.

"Ladies and gentlemen, I'm not saying that Regnāre stole medicine from old people, and that his exterior is made from the skins of cute puppies, and that somewhere far away infants are starving so that he can live in luxury, and I'm not saying that by supporting him you are responsible for old people not having medicine, puppies not having skin, and faraway infants not having food, but I'm not *not* saying that, either."

Of course, the accusations I didn't quite make were baseless. Not that it really mattered what I said. Studies have conclusively demonstrated that 89% of winning an argument is talking louder than the other guy. I talked way louder than the other guy. People didn't know whether they agreed with me, or what exactly I had said that might or might not be agreed with. They still didn't know what I was doing on stage. All they knew was that Regnāre was somehow involved with stealing medicine from old people, and hurting puppies, and starving infants, and they felt that somehow it was their own fault. They didn't want to believe it, but what they wanted to believe didn't influence the score. Regnāre's points came off the board faster than they had accumulated. Three seconds later, the old-people-medicine-robbing, puppy-harming, infant-starving champion had no points at all.

A class B hullabaloo set in. Regnāre never lost and the gamblers always won, but Regnāre had lost. Anachron had won with a measly four points. All the bets on Regnāre were losers. Celebrating people had spent lots of money on champagne, which they now tried to return for a full refund. There was shouting. Someone swatted a betbot out of the air. The private back doors opened as dozens of Win-Fall security guards rushed the Argumania floor to prevent the level-three ruckus from going right past fracas and becoming an all-out melee.

Tommy Ten-Toes called himself that because he had ten toes. It was true that pretty much everyone else also had ten toes, but that didn't make it less true that Tommy did. Although Tommy Ten-Toes had ten fingers as well, he never considered calling himself Tommy Ten-Fingers. He wasn't at all ashamed of having ten fingers. It just wasn't something he wanted to be known for. Why he wanted to be known for having ten toes was a secret he shared with no one, not that anyone was brave enough to ask. No, Tommy Ten-Toes wasn't exactly the sort of man who would cut off your fingers for the slightest perceived insult. He was, however, exactly the sort of man who would order someone else to do so.

Of course, no one asking, and no one answering what wasn't asked, only made speculation rampant. Theories abounded, as they are wont to do when speculation is rampant. They multiplied, not like rabbits, because though they abounded, they didn't exactly hop. They more spread like wildfire. Not as hot or fiery, to be sure, but still plenty wild and carried away by the wind. No one dared tell Tommy Ten-Toes about the speculation or the theories for the same reason no one asked him why he called himself Tommy Ten-Toes. And no one had to tell him—Tommy Ten-Toes always knew that people talked about his name. He was counting on it.[55]

A popular theory was that growing up on the rough streets outside the Great American was what had made Tommy so tough. Times were desperate out there and with an empty stomach and an emptier conscience, little Tommy resorted to eating people's toes to survive. Yes, their toes. It was said that he had eaten hundreds of toes throughout his childhood but was called Ten-Toes because that's how many constituted a typical meal. Although he now lived in the Great American with abundant food supplies, some believed he hadn't lost his digital tastes. It was for this reason that you never saw anyone wearing sandals or open-toed shoes of any kind in his presence. While there was no evidence to support the tale of toe consumption, it did qualify as conjecture and was therefore taken quite seriously by people who took it seriously, as most things are.

Another popular theory was that Tommy was born with twelve toes instead of the expected ten (an extra pinky toe on each foot), and lived the first six years of his life being told to hide his feet from the other children, who his parents thought would tease him. His family was unable to find a doctor to remove the extra appendages because of the extraordinary circumstances outside the Great American in those days, and six-year-old Tommy finally took foot matters into his own hands and cut off his superfluous toes with a very sharp butcher's knife. The extreme act of cutting off one's own extremities transformed Tommy into the man he became, and from that day forward he called himself Tommy Ten-Toes to remind himself what it took to succeed. Also, he called himself that to make sure everyone else knew he had the ordinary number of toes, since his unrefined surgical technique had left dramatic scars and,

---

[55] Which he finally revealed in his disjointed memoir, *The Nine Lives of Tommy Ten-Toes*, published posthumously ninety-two years later, when he said on page 131, "I was counting on it."

even with the perfect number of toes, he refused to wear sandals or let his feet be seen.

Even more popular was the theory that Tommy had once had a dispute with Big-Toes McGee, the outside criminal underworld's most feared enforcer. It was no secret at all why McGee was called Big-Toes. He had enormous toes. Freakishly large. Bigger than whatever size you might be imagining, even if your imagination is delirious and silly. No shoes ever made could cover his toes, and Big-Toes McGee wouldn't have worn them anyway. His big toes were his calling cards, except they weren't cards but toes, and he didn't leave them behind, and they didn't have contact information on them—they were actually nothing like calling cards, which was just as well, since it had been many decades since anyone had handed out actual business cards to get others to call. But though they were not calling cards, they were nevertheless what made him known far and wide (not as wide as his toes, but still pretty wide) as Big-Toes McGee. Every day, he wore the same sandals that showcased his horribly humongous mutant toes.

To keep a short story short, let's just say that the dispute ended with Big-Toes McGee sporting ten large toe casts for ten broken toes after Tommy stomped on his feet while wearing iron boots. After breaking all ten mighty toes of the feared Big-Toes McGee, sending him into retirement, Tommy took his rightful place as a feared crime lord and was forever after known as Tommy Ten-Toes. It's true that no one could confirm this story. Nor could anyone be certain that, in fact, Big-Toes McGee had ever existed. It was even less certain what brand of sandals McGee had liked to wear. Still, many people enjoyed the story, maybe because someone stomping on a person's toes is generally considered hilarious as long as the toes do not belong to you.

A fourth theory, gaining in popularity in recent months, was that Tommy Ten-Toes spent the first seventeen years of his life not knowing how to count because of a terrible fear of hands that prevented him from adding numbers on his own fingers or anyone else's. When told to try counting on his toes, he had said, "Toes are the fingers of the foot." He reasoned that if feet had fingers called *toes*, they were sort of like hands, and then feet began to scare him almost as much as hands did. It was only after months of intensive therapy consisting of alternating electric shocks and being dunked in cold buckets of water that he finally overcame his fear of feet and, indeed, learned to count his ten toes, which was the beginning of the end of his fear of fingers as well. Soon he could count to twenty using all of his fingers and toes, and from there, naturally, he went on to a brilliant life of crime, as one would expect.

There were other theories, some emerging and still seeking supporters, some around for years and never quite catching on but never quite fading away, some the result of late-night poker conversations unremembered and lost to history, others half-remembered but still forgotten. The vast criminal network Tommy Ten-Toes ruled talked of little else. Which is just how Tommy wanted it. Incessant discussion of his name kept his minions in awe of him and prevented any disobedience, but that was only a secondary benefit.

Tommy's genius was his deep understanding of human beings and the limits of their brains. The real reason he had named himself Tommy Ten-Toes from the very beginning, the reason he planted rumors and counter-rumors, the reason he secretly smiled as people argued over theories and whispered in hushed tones, the reason he not only tolerated unheard jokes but covertly encouraged them, was that focusing everyone's attention on his name made it unlikely—impossible, really—for anyone to notice that he had only one nostril.

It was a masterstroke of misdirection. A man with one nostril might face a lifetime of teasing, might have a difficult time rising through the ranks and commanding the respect of his underlings, but a man with ten toes and a mythology to match could accomplish great things.

Frank Harken looked Tommy Ten-Toes straight on, risking dizziness. Though Ten-Toes was facing Harken, one could be forgiven for thinking he was facing the far wall on the left—looking at Tommy Ten-Toes was like staring too long at a Picasso profile. The more you looked, the less sure you were of what you were seeing. As if endeavoring to make the task even more difficult, Ten-Toes wore a magnificent black and white checkered suit with a black and white checkered tie and shirt and very shiny black and white checkered shoes, a large crimson-pink flower pinned to his lapel. He was the handsomest kitchen floor ever.[56]

Harken looked at me and frowned. I don't know why he frowned. I was pleased. Harken had said he wanted the guards away from the back door. He had said that it would be even better if someone would open the door for us. I had surpassed reasonable expectations for both requests. Not only had I lured the guards from the door, but I had also lured many other guards from the room on the other side of the door. Not only had someone opened the door for us, but in the total duration of a mere fifty-seven seconds, thirty-two someones had rushed out, twenty to quell the class B hullabaloo and a dozen to grab us and hustle us through the open doors into the private backroom and then close the doors again. I'd had us hand-delivered to the exact location Harken wanted to reach. If anything, he should have been thanking me for my superb service instead of shaking his head and frowning at me like I was a dog who had peed in his slippers before fetching them.

Ten-Toes was also frowning and shaking his head. The sight was enough to cause disorientation. That's why it took a moment for Harken to realize that Ten-Toes was not frowning and shaking his head at us. He was frowning and shaking his head at the aftermath of a fight in the backroom, a fight that had gone badly for the four unconscious men sprawled on the burgundy carpet and billiards table. When the thirty-two guards had rushed out of the backroom to snatch me and Harken and prevent an all-out melee at Argumania, four had remained

---

[56] Not officially. The Great American Kitchen Floor Awards weren't being announced for another two months.

behind with Tommy Ten-Toes. In the mere fifty-seven seconds the guards were gone collecting us, the beautiful assailant had swooped from the ceiling, flipping, punching, and kicking through four guards in a whirlwind frenzy before snatching Pretty Lovely and escaping through a cloaked ceiling hatch.[57] Besides the unconscious men, broken cue sticks and a shattered glass coffee table were the only visible evidence left by the unknown attacker. There was the faint scent of cake in the air. It smelled delicious.

"Iceberg!" Ten-Toes yelled. "Iceberg, get in here!"

In lumbered the hairy glacier we'd encountered at Lettuce Snow. His puffy white coat from earlier was gone. He wore the largest white tuxedo you've ever seen and an extra-large white bowtie. His shoulders had shoulders. From within his shirt, sandy hair struggled like weeds through the top of his collar and bloomed into a hirsute garden all around his neck. His kind face had deep-set eyes the color of an arctic ocean that wasn't even a little polluted.

"What is it, boss?" Iceberg had a gentle voice. You might call it timid if you weren't too busy being scared he would accidentally crush you to death.

"What is it?" Tommy Ten-Toes asked. "What is it? Look around."

Iceberg looked around. "Someone broke our cue sticks. Oh, and the coffee table."

Ten-Toes had yet to stop frowning. "And four of our guys! And stole our guest! Where the hell were you?"

"I had to use the bathroom."

"What is the point of having a man-mountain enforcer if he's going to be in the bathroom when an assassin attacks?"

"I didn't know an assassin was going to attack." Iceberg was apologetic.

---

[57] I easily reconstructed the scene from the trail left by the tracking ring's signature.

"Of course you didn't. Assassins don't announce when they're going to attack.[58] You're always going to the bathroom at the worst times."

"Boss, I drank that entire tub of soda you got me. My bladder was full."

"What are you talking about? I didn't get you a tub of soda."

"Are you sure? I'm talking about the tub of soda you left for me on the bar. It had a big note on it that said, *For Iceberg, You're doing a great job. Enjoy this entire tub of soda. Fondly, Tommy Ten-Toes.* It was very nice of you to get my favorite flavor, cherry red."

"Iceberg, listen to me carefully. I did not get you a tub of soda! I definitely did not leave a note on it telling you you're doing a great job! I sure as hell did not know your favorite flavor! Someone must have put the soda there and forged a note from me. Use your head! Next time, don't go to the bathroom when an assassin is about to strike!"

"But my bladder was full." There was a hint of pleading in his voice.

"For what I pay you, you can hold it in."

Iceberg didn't think holding it in was a reasonable option, but he relented. It wasn't wise to argue with Tommy Ten-Toes. "Yes, boss." Then he saw Harken. "Hey, where'd he come from?"

"I don't have time to fill you in on the details every time you take a potty break," Ten-Toes said. "You remember our old friend, Detective Frank Harken? The insignificant gnat who once accused me of hijacking trucks? He's in cahoots with the assassin."

Harken had heard enough. "In cahoots? I'm not in cahoots with anyone."

"Is that so?" Ten-Toes asked Harken. "I suppose it's just a coincidence that you caused the commotion that required most of my guards to leave, allowing the assassin to strike."

Harken had caught the scent of cake, knew there was only one person who could have gotten to Pretty Lovely before we

---

[58] Assassins were notoriously inconsiderate.

did. It was obvious that Nutella had left an entire tub of soda on the bar for Iceberg, perfectly timed to send him to the bathroom just before our ruckus gave her the opportunity to attack. Nutella must have been waiting for a distraction to make her move. Our class B hullabaloo was just what she'd needed. "I'm not a big believer in coincidences."

"Aha! So you are in cahoots with the assassin!"

"I work alone."

My "ahem" was effective.

Harken corrected himself. "Excuse me. *We* work alone."

I handed him a coffee. His casual sipping and satisfied smile pushed Ten-Toes way past annoyed. We were surrounded by a dozen guards, and Iceberg stood at Ten-Toes' side. Now did not seem to be the ideal time to be disagreeable. As Harken would later tell me, there was rarely an ideal time to be disagreeable, which was why he wasn't much of an idealist. "And why do you keep calling the attacker an *assassin*? These four men are very much alive."

Ten-Toes did not want a vocabulary lesson. "So are you. For now."

"Are you threatening me?" Harken wasn't used to being pushed around.

"Yes," Ten-Toes said.

"You think I'm scared of you because you're Tommy Ten-Toes, organized crime boss?"

"That's where you're wrong, detective. I *was* Tommy Ten-Toes, organized crime boss. In here, there is no organized crime. The rackets is no way to make a living in the Great American. Now I'm Tommy Ten-Toes, wildly successful entrepreneur, casino magnate, and all-around upstanding nice guy."

"You expect me to believe you've gone straight?"

"Gone straight? What are you, a moron? I'm Tommy Ten-Toes. I don't go straight. What I said was the rackets is no way to make a living in here. You can't run an organized crime outfit like I did in the old days, out there. It's a shame so few things are illegal in the Great American. About the only thing left to sell on the black market is peanut butter, but when we tried to smuggle some in, we lost a half-dozen men to anaphylactic shock due to allergic reaction. Anyway, in here there's more money to be made in legal entertainment. The Win-Fall chain does more business than any network of hoods hijacking trucks could ever hope for."

"It sounds like a tough time to be a crook. I'm glad it hasn't prevented you from buying checkered suits."

"My tailor shares your gladness." Ten-Toes poured himself a stiff drink and tilted his glass back and forth to let thick amber liquid work through the ice cubes. "It's nice to see you again, detective. Remember the good old days, those couple of times you tried busting me on the outside? Is that why you're here now? Still trying to put me away?"

"Ten-Toes, I didn't come here to reminisce about the good old days. I know you kidnapped Pretty Lovely. Tell me what you want with her. Tell me what you did with Winsome Smiles."

"I didn't do anything with Winsome Smiles. I'm looking for her, same as you. You might be able to see that if you weren't blinded by your vendetta for me. Besides, you're not in any position[59] to be making demands."

Harken considered the massive tuxedoed man and the dozen sport-coated guards and slowly drank more coffee. Even without my computational prowess, he calculated that these weren't the best odds for fisticuffs. "I left the past in the past, where it belongs. I'm not here on any vendetta. I'm here on a case, followed the evidence where it led. Just tell me what you want with Winsome Smiles, and I'll be on my way."

"I'll tell you what's going to happen, detective. I will let you go and permit you to keep all of your limbs, and my man Iceberg will go with you. You're looking for Winsome Smiles. So am I. When you find her, I find her."

"I need to know what you want with Winsome Smiles."

"Iceberg will accompany you. That's all you need to know."

---

[59] Harken's position was relaxed and slightly slouched. We were not told what position would be better for making demands, though that information would have been helpful.

Harken wasn't used to taking orders. "And if I refuse?"

Tommy Ten-Toes smiled, an unsettling sight. He spoke without malice. "If you refuse, my man Iceberg will squash you like a tiny gnat here and now."

Our new friend, Iceberg, had been walking in silence for six minutes and fourteen seconds. I rolled alongside Frank Harken, who also walked in silence. I was not physiologically wired to experience an actual itch, on account of my lack of skin and nerve endings, but I was itching to talk. A bot programmed for stimulating conversation can only tolerate mute companions for so long before the urge to scratch becomes overwhelming.

"If I may inquire, why are you called *Iceberg*? Is it because you like lettuce? If so, why not name yourself *Romaine*? It contains far more nutrients. Or why not name yourself *Greenleaf*? Are you allergic to Vitamin K? In that case, iceberg would make more sense than Greenleaf. Otherwise, iceberg really isn't the most efficient use of farmland, though I have heard that for some reason people enjoy the crunching sound it makes when chewed."

Our new friend, Iceberg, didn't answer me. Neither he nor Harken seemed pleased to be walking with the other. Despite having their reciprocal dislike in common, they had yet to become inseparable pals for life. Twelve seconds of quiet had passed. It was all I could take.

"I don't mean to pry," I said, prying. "Are you called *Iceberg* because you really enjoy the cold? If so, I can understand that. One of my closest friends is a refrigerator."[60]

No response. Harken glanced at me sideways, shook his head, said nothing. Our stroll through Blue Neighborhood 261 took us past four mini-golf courses (dinosaurs, invasive surgery, dead celebrities, pirates). A food court up ahead was beginning the night session. Lawyers were preparing to deliver opening statements. Dining jurors carrying trays of food jockeyed[61] for tables with good views of the proceedings. Nine seconds of quiet had passed. I scratched the itch.

"Pardon me, but are you called *Iceberg* because one time many years ago, when you were cooking frozen burgers for friends, you didn't heat the burgers enough and the meat was still solid ice when you served the food, and dinner was ruined and they all decided to tease you by calling you *Iceburger*? And then, years later, you shortened it to *Iceberg* to hide your shame? If so, I am sorry for bringing up such a painful memory."

Iceberg didn't answer. Harken did.

"Arjay! Ease up on the ludicrous questions. Can't you see that he's obviously called *Iceberg* because he's gigantic and wears all white? Just look at him. He's as big as a freakin' iceberg. You don't want to be an unsinkable cruise ship anywhere near this guy."

Iceberg was quiet another moment, then softly said, "That hurt. Your words are hurtful, Frank Harken. If you must know, I wear white because it's slimming.[62] I'm more than merely a giant brute. As a matter of fact, I named myself *Iceberg* because what you see on the surface is but a minuscule fraction of who I am."

---

[60] I missed that appliance. It knew how to make conversation.

[61] There was no escaping thinking about horses.

[62] White is not slimming, but this didn't seem like an appropriate time to point out the flaws in Iceberg's fashion knowledge.

"Oh," Harken said. "Hmm. Um, no offense intended. You know, though, you *are* very big, and you *are* wearing all white, and you *are* called *Iceberg*. It was a reasonable deduction."

Iceberg spoke more softly. "You have wounded me. I am wounded."

"I didn't mean to. How was I supposed to know I was walking with the world's most sensitive enforcer?"

A cold tear fell from Iceberg's arctic eye.

"Well, now I feel bad. I've never made an indestructible glacier cry before." His words might look sarcastic, but they had a conciliatory tone.

"It's okay," Iceberg said. "I'm fine."

It was a terribly awkward moment for the humans, I suppose. It didn't bother me. I was just happy everyone was talking. After another brief silent stretch, conversation shifted to the next crucial task: dinner.

We were already in the food court, a small one by Great American standards. It had only sixty-one eateries and two pretzel kiosks. A mere nineteen cases were on the evening docket. Harken watched three particularly indecisive molk go from one establishment to another, then back again, then back to the second, then back to the first, then back to the second—forty-three times—unable to settle on which of the two places had the tastier-looking barbecued chicken vegetable lo mein. The first place had greener broccoli, but the second place had oranger carrots. They debated the merits of the two lo meins, quoting from customer reviews and ratings from connected diners who were currently enjoying (or not enjoying) the lo meins in question. Sources were inconclusive about which lo mein was better. It was a real dilemma.

Harken wanted to eat anywhere but the food court. Perhaps he didn't like lo mein. Either that, or he hated justice.

Iceberg didn't want to eat at all. He was still full from the kale salad[63] he'd consumed earlier at Lettuce Snow. Besides, he was watching his calories because some people (not naming any

---

[63] No mention was made of drinking an entire tub of cherry red soda.

names) thought it was amusing to make fun of his largeness. I didn't consume food and was therefore neutral on the matters of whether and where to have dinner. However, I reminded Frank Harken that we were on a case and minutes counted. He tapped his wristwatch and said he knew all about minutes counting, but dinner counted, too. I didn't know what that meant, and I don't think he did, either. When humans are hungry, they have trouble making sense.

Mad Monk's was notable for being an ordinary restaurant. There were no trials taking place. This resulted in a distinct absence of booing jurors. Not a single person was dressed as a tremendous meatball. The establishment was at 63% of its seating capacity of 242 persons. Fingers at the bar's piano danced over "Straight, No Chaser." Wearing a gray suit and skinny black tie, the pianist bebopped with such ferocity, his knitted beret nearly flew from his head. Plastered all around Mad Monk's walls were reproductions of jazz album[64] covers. The hanging lamp above our booth was a translucent saxophone giving off very little light, like every other lamp in the place, but that didn't stop all the waiters and bartenders from wearing sunglasses.

Iceberg hadn't lied—there sure was a lot more to him than you saw at first glance. When he squeezed into the booth and sat across from Harken, his bulk moved the table 3.74 inches in Harken's direction. "I don't know why you insisted on getting a booth."

Harken still had plenty of room on his side of the table. "I like them better than chairs. People are less likely to pick up a booth and hit you over the head with it."

"You have a violent imagination. People aren't so bad in here," Iceberg said.

---

[64] It is widely believed that albums were fragile, ancient discs people threw to each other at picnics, which is why so few of them survive despite having been kept in elaborately decorated protective sleeves.

Harken laughed. "Violent imagination? That's real funny coming from a thumb-breaker."

"Who said I broke thumbs?"

"I just assumed."

"You make a lot of assumptions. Have you seen me break anyone's thumbs? Show me one thumb I've broken. Just one."

It was the first time Harken had seen Iceberg upset. The table shook. Also, the walls. "Calm down, calm down. Okay, if you don't break people's thumbs, then what do you break? Kneecaps?"

Iceberg had calmed down, was quietly offended. "I don't break anything."

"Aren't you Tommy Ten-Toes' enforcer?"

"I am. Have been for almost four years, since he came to the Great American. That doesn't mean I break people's thumbs."

"Or kneecaps," I helpfully added.

"Or kneecaps," Iceberg agreed. "When you're as big as I am, violence isn't necessary very often. Showing up is all the enforcement you need. I haven't had to break anything yet."

"It's good to know you're a pacifist," Harken said.

Iceberg's quiet voice grew serious. "I said *yet*. Don't mistake my gentle manner for pacifism. I don't want to hurt anyone. Not even you, Frank Harken, though you continue to insult me. But I have a job to do, bills to pay like everyone else. I'll squash you like a tiny gnat if I have no other choice. Trust me—I can break things if I need to."

"I don't doubt it," Harken said. "I think you're breaking the booth."

"So that's how it's going to be? More jokes about my size?"

"Sorry," Harken said, "You can't throw a grapefruit over the plate like that and expect me to lay off."

"I have no idea what that means,[65] but I don't expect you to see past the surface of my appearance. I'm more than a mere brute."

It's possible the tension was thick enough to cut with a knife, but our waiter had not yet brought eating utensils, so we couldn't know for sure. Lightening the mood required my vast interpersonal expertise. "Perhaps you could tell us more about what you do when you aren't not breaking thumbs and knee-caps."

"You don't want to hear about that." Iceberg was bashful.

"I certainly do." I certainly did.

"It isn't very interesting."

"I think everything is fascinating."

Harken said, "It's true. You should hear Arjay go on and on about the Great American's innovative water filtration system. It'll fascinate you right to death."

"I'll tell you about it some time," I promised Iceberg. "But right now we want to learn more about you."

"Really?" Iceberg was asking Harken. I was hopeful. We were on the verge of an interpersonal breakthrough.

"Sure," Harken finally said. "What the hell. It can't be worse than hearing about Great American innovations in waste re-moval."

"If you insist." Iceberg mustered some enthusiasm. "As I've said, there's a lot more to me than meets the eye. All people see is a behemoth, but most don't know about my many interests and hobbies."

"For example?" Harken asked, almost pretending to care.

"I really like watching the sunset."[66]

---

[65] Harken might have been referring to an obscure sport played many years ago consisting mainly of standing around and spitting, though what that had to do with citrus fruit is unclear.

[66] There were limited opportunities to see the sunset in the Great American. He was most likely referring to viewing vids of the sun setting, a popular pastime at all times of day, often accompanied by Bordeaux and cheese.

"Fascinating," I said. "Tell us more."

"And I'm something of a fashion buff. As you might guess by looking at me, I was one of the first to get body hair implants when the natural look became the in thing a few years ago."

I admired the neck hair framing his tuxedoed shoulders. "It's a shame that trend didn't last very long."

"Yeah. The implants are pretty expensive to remove. You never know, though. It might become popular again. Fashion can be fickle."

"You're really an intriguing man," I said. "What else?"

"I also enjoy the poetry of Paul Neil Milne Johnstone."

"You don't meet many enforcers who like poetry," Harken said.

"I wasn't always an enforcer. I had other jobs."

"Were you ever a dentist? Not possessing one myself, I find the mouth a fascinating orifice, especially the teeth part of the mouth."

"Dentist?"

"Yes. At Lettuce Snow, Pretty Lovely told GAS you were her dentist. Frank Harken said she was lying."

"Oh, that. No, I was never a dentist. She just said that to get GAS to back off. Tommy Ten-Toes had warned her about bringing them into this. Coincidentally, though, I actually studied to be a dental hygienist a few years back."

"Really?"

"Absolutely. I thought it would be a secure career, something that wouldn't go automated too soon. People don't trust bots to wield sharp cleaning implements in their mouths, for good reason.[67] I wish it had worked out. I think I would have liked cleaning people's teeth. I enjoyed my three days of hygienist school before I was asked to leave."

Harken seemed genuinely interested. "Why were you asked to leave?"

---

[67] One malfunctioning dentalbot performs an unscheduled radical tonsillectomy, and for decades the rest can't live down the bad publicity. Imagine if humans were held to this standard.

Iceberg held up his hand. It was bigger than a cantaloupe.[68] "No one wanted one of these in their mouth."

Harken nodded. "I can see that being a problem. What I can't see is how you go from wanting to clean people's teeth to making a living knocking them out."

"You don't listen so good. I've already said that I don't have to engage in violence to do this job."

"Come on, Iceberg. You must know that intimidating people with your size will only go so far. You say it's worked up till now, but at some point, in your line of work, you're gonna hit someone. That someone is probably gonna lose a lot of teeth. I guess you could clean the teeth after you knock them out. Which is good timing, 'cause they'll be covered in blood."

Iceberg probably would have retorted something to the effect that he didn't knock out people's teeth, and could Harken show him even one tooth he knocked out, and there was more to him than being a mere brute. However, he didn't have the chance to say any of it because just then the waiter brought dinner to the table. Iceberg and Harken hadn't ordered any food nor looked at a menu, yet neither was surprised at the arrival of their smoked brisket and baked beans. Mad Monk's never cooked anything else. If you could taste the brisket and beans, you'd understand why that was just fine with its customers, who never tired of the limited menu. The improvisational chef was a culinary genius admired for never making the same dish twice, even though she never made anything but the same dish. There wasn't much talking after the food arrived.

As full as Iceberg was from the kale salad earlier in the day, he managed to eat all of the brisket and beans on his heaping plate. Harken had a healthy appetite as well and finished close to a third of his. Dinner passed with only a minor incident toward the meal's end, involving my almost having to sever a waiter's hand from his wrist for trying to serve a cup of coffee to Frank Harken. *That* was my job. Wisely, the waiter decided that

---

[68] Which was quite a bit larger than a grapefruit and much, much larger than a kumquat.

he could make an exception to the no-bringing-your-own-food-or-beverages-into-the-restaurant policy, and I let him go and deactivated my vibrational saw and gave Harken a truly sublime cup of coffee.

Iceberg had already seen me ski. He sipped the adequate immensely inferior coffee the waiter had provided. "That's some coffeemaker you have there. Is there anything it can't do?"

Harken shrugged and breathed in his own superior steaming coffee. "I don't know. Why don't you try squashing me like a tiny gnat? We might just find out."

"Where are we going?"

Frank Harken didn't answer Iceberg. He wasn't happy about the crush[69] of people crammed into our shuttle car. The magnetic rail was the quickest method of travel to mid-distant neighborhoods, and now that he'd eaten, minutes counted again, so Harken tolerated the crowd heading to dance clubs, dinner, breakfast, card games, game shows, shoe sales, pickling exhibitions, romantic liaisons, mini-golf, earring parties, beer tastings, and psychic readings. After a minute and forty-eight seconds of frictionless cruising down the center of shopping level B, the shuttle stopped and we exited in Turquoise Neighborhood 291.

"Harken, I'd like to know where we're going."

"You'll find out when we get there."

Iceberg pouted. "You are unnecessarily difficult."

"I know. It's one of this gig's few joys." He relished the lack of conversation that followed as we walked for three minutes

---

[69] *Crush* had a density factor 16.1% greater than *throng*.

and thirteen seconds. I was unaccustomedly unperturbed by the silence, because I knew where we were going and literally couldn't have been more full of anticipation.[70]

We entered Mauve Neighborhood 289 and up ahead saw the Great American Zoo. The sign at the entrance assured us, *It's a zoo in here!* And what a zoo it was, the third largest in the Great American, one of the most popular interactivity destinations in Western Region Fourteen. People loved the zoo. I wasn't a person, but maybe I would love the zoo, too. I had never seen a real, live animal before, but even images and vids stimulated my cuteness receptors. The zoo was the only attraction that occupied the main concourse as well as the shopping district store space. Shuttles and the moving residential district above bypassed the zoo. However, if you wanted to continue walking in any of the four levels of the shopping district's main concourse, you had to go through. Since I'd never been to a Great American Zoo before, I had many questions for Frank Harken.

Would we see a tiger there? How many stripes would it have? Would we see a zebra there? How many stripes would it have? Would we see a kangaroo there? Could I peek in its pouch? Would we see a giraffe there?[71] How tall would it be? Would we see a gorilla there? Would it know sign language and, if it did, what did Harken think it would say? Nothing obscene, I hoped. Would we see those little spider monkeys there? Would we see a giant anaconda there? Would small children be allowed to ride it? Would we see an alligator there? Would we see a crocodile there? Would people be able to tell the alligator and the crocodile apart? Would the alligator and the crocodile have a confusing, forbidden friendship none of the other animals knew about? Would we see a black bear there? Would it ride a bicycle, or did that only happen in zoos back in ancient times?

---

[70] I was at 100% capacity. Any additional anticipation would have had to wait until I'd deployed some of my current supply.

[71] I meant at the zoo, not in the kangaroo's pouch. Unless the giraffe was tiny.

"Arjay, no more questions. Please."

Iceberg shook his head, likely at Harken, possibly at me. "The zoo? What are we doing at the zoo?"

"That's where Arjay said Pretty Lovely is."

"When did he say that?"

"At Mad Monk's."

"I don't remember hearing him say anything about the zoo."

"Arjay told me after we'd finished dinner, while you were in the bathroom. That's when I decided the zoo would be our next stop."

"Why didn't you include me in the discussion? You could have waited for me to come back, you know."

"It seems that you're always going to the bathroom at the worst times." Harken was enjoying himself.

Iceberg appeared to finally recognize that his frequently full bladder was becoming an occupational liability. Perhaps he shouldn't have consumed an entire tub of soda with his Mad Monk's meal and then topped it off with a coffee.

"Maybe I *am* always going to the bathroom at the worst times, Harken. Maybe I am. That doesn't mean we should leave all the decisions to a coffeemaker."

"I don't leave all the decisions to a coffeemaker. Just the important ones."

It's possible[72] I blushed.

Iceberg said he wasn't happy to play second fiddle[73] to an appliance. A bit of my interpersonal expertise was needed to ease the awkwardness. I changed the subject. "Iceberg, do you think we'll see a herd of antelope there?"

Iceberg ignored my question. He might not have shared my enthusiasm for touring the zoo. "What do we care where Pretty

---

[72] Actually, it isn't.

[73] He didn't have to worry about that because we weren't playing musical instruments at all. Moreover, in the event a musical performance became necessary, he would play third fiddle (at best), since Harken and I would play the first two.

Lovely is, anyway? We're not looking for her. We're looking for Winsome Smiles. That's all Ten-Toes is interested in."

Harken wasn't having any of that. "I don't work for Tommy Ten-Toes. I'm looking for both of them. And besides, Pretty might know something that would help us find Winsome."

Iceberg disagreed. "Ten-Toes asked her plenty of questions already. She doesn't know anything."

Harken didn't care what Iceberg thought. He hadn't asked for his opinion. And he certainly didn't need another partner. "Iceberg, you let me do the detecting, and I'll let you do the being-larger-than-a-continental-mass."

Iceberg seemed to ignore this insult. Beneath the surface, though, where there was much more to him than met the eye, I think being left out of the let's-go-to-the-zoo discussion had deeply injured the gentle giant. Wounded him, even. I suppose that's why I never did find out his antelope expectations.

This branch of the Great American Zoo covered 383 acres on a total of four levels of the shopping district. It was a marvel of naturescaping. Like a traditional zoo from olden times, it was divided into sections based on natural habitats of the animals—jungle, plains, metropolitan, forest, desert, suburban, frozen tundra, swamp, so on. Unlike zoos from those unenlightened days, people didn't walk freely on paved paths and gape at animals stuck in glorified cages. In the Great American Zoo, the people were the ones in cages and the animals roamed free in their spacious habitats, authentically simulated to the last detail.

Hundreds of transparent cubes suspended from multiple tracks glided through each ginormous habitat. Our cube was fifteen feet long, ten feet wide, and eight feet high, and contained a circular bench in its center. People in the cube could sit on the bench facing any direction they chose or could stand and hold the handrails at the cube's edge for a more personal encounter with the wild. This was no perimeter monorail ride that only let people view animals from afar. The automated paths on which the cubes traveled shifted in response to the location of the animals. Gone were the savage days of zoos of yore, when people had to stand around and wait for an animal to make an appearance if it felt like it. Back then, you could spend half a day staring at a tree and not once see a single panda bear and, for reasons murky at best, *not get a refund*. Fortunately for Great American Zoo visitors, that horror was in the past.

The cubes homed in on the animals people wanted to see. It was common to glide right up to lascivious lions or sleepy sloths. Many of the animals here had long ago given up trying to maintain any semblance of a private life. The wild beasts went right on lasciviousing and sleeping even as the cube brushed up against them. Don't feel bad for the animals. What did they have to hide, anyway? Besides, usually the people didn't pay much attention to the intimate goings-on. Most of their attention was spent on captioning the vid moment with a pithy comment they could share with connected friends.

Harken and Iceberg stood at the front of the cube-car, much to the displeasure of 33.333% of the six other occupants. Parents and their four young children could not see where we were going because of world history's largest white tuxedo blocking their view. It's a good thing the cube was clear on all sides and the top and bottom. There were unobstructed views of the jungle forest in every other direction. Two of the children didn't care either way. They were immersed in a lens game and didn't know a humongous man blocked their view, or that they were in a zoo, or that our cube was almost touching a tiger mama nursing her cubs.

Tigers! Tiger cubs! Nursing tiger cubs! It was too much. I started to spin and shout, "Animals!" My full anticipation erupted and overflowed, nearly flooding my cooling chamber.

"Arjay!" Harken yelled. "Settle down. You're frightening the children."

Two of the children stared, far more intrigued by me than by the tigers. You'd think they'd never seen a coffeemaker before. The other two continued their lens games, not aware of me or the nursing tigers two feet away. Their connected parents perused photos of their friends' dinners and played word games against faraway opponents. I hardly think I frightened anyone. The mother tiger swiped at our cube, though that could be because she liked us. I didn't have enough data to conclude anything with confidence. It was my first big cat encounter. Regretfully, I neglected to count the number of stripes on the tigers. I was quite flustered.

Emergency filters purged my anticipation lines and I returned to my usual, level demeanor. After we saw tigers, we entered the plains and saw a herd of zebra. They had 513 stripes.[74] Then we saw a giraffe. It was 18.72 feet tall and definitely would not have fit in the pouch of even the exceptionally developed specimen of a kangaroo mother we saw later, who, to my surprise and disappointment, was not eager to let me peek in her pouch. This, despite my asking politely as our cube passed above a mob of fourteen kangaroos in the outback habitat. Maybe she didn't understand English, being Australian.

The gorillas we met were no better—they didn't know any sign language and couldn't form a single word.[75] Spider monkeys communicated plenty, by throwing more feces at us than decorum required. Fortunately, our cube was self-cleaning and sprayed itself with soapy water as we left the tropical rainforest. Unfortunately for the well-fed small children, we never did see a giant anaconda. We did briefly encounter an alligator or a crocodile. No one seemed to know which. The reptile was submerged and antisocial. If a black bear was riding a bicycle in the woods, we couldn't tell. The forest was inconveniently thick with trees. We did see a bear doing something else in the woods, which was no surprise—we'd always assumed that's where bears did that.

We entered the metropolitan habitat, perfectly scaped to match the appearance of a three-block stretch of a 21st-century

---

[74] Depending on what you count as a stripe and your acuity of vision, adjust that to 989, 454, or seven.

[75] Ape illiteracy is pervasive and sad.

city. Majestic pigeons flew all about. Cute rats scurried through and around piles and piles of uncollected black trash bags on the sidewalk. Rambunctious raccoons climbed from street sinkholes, careful to avoid overgrown ball pythons wrapped around streetlamp bases. Our cube elevated and passed through the fifth floor of a glass and steel high-rise building. The exhibit containing 138,493 cockroaches in a full-scale apartment kitchen was most informative. Maybe that's why two children in our cube started to scream. Information is exciting.

The most dangerous habitat we visited was the suburbs. Deer kept darting in front of our cube, daring us to crash into them. We had to stop short seven times to avoid an unpleasant accident. More frightening still were the squirrels, scourge of gardens throughout the civilized world. They scampered like they owned the place, tearing tulips from their stems and breaking into squirrel-proof bird feeders, scattering decapitated flowers and stolen seed over meticulously manicured lawns. I can't say for sure that the squirrels were sending us a warning with this gruesome display, but I wouldn't put it past them.

Our suburban adventure concluded with our cube gliding through a replica of a giant home improvement warehouse retail store. We saw cardinals, bluejays, and sparrows flying in the rafters. A bluejay relentlessly harassed[76] the other birds and stole their food until several cardinals teamed up and chased it off. Then they all nestled in for the night, snug in their nests high above the shiny lawnmowers and barbecue grills on the sales floor below.

The cube let us off in the kiddie zoo, where families and children could get even more up close and personal with shows, hands-on activities, and specially designed rare wild beasts. The family of six from our cube headed to the sweater barn to shear

---

[76] It was the general consensus of ornithologists that bluejays are the biggest jerks in the animal kingdom. Suburban gardeners might have argued that squirrels are worse. They were both right. (Unless humans are considered part of the animal kingdom, in which case the biggest jerk was Roger Smith from East Dakota. No one liked that guy.)

a yak. They were going to make an afghan for grandma's birthday. She always said a person can never have too many afghans whenever they gave her one, which is why, to her annual delight, they made her a new afghan every year. Two of the children complained that they didn't want to touch a smelly yak. The other two were nearing their high scores in Drone Attack and were neither for nor against touching a smelly yak. Their eyes were blank, and their heads swayed slightly as they piloted virtual drones. I was going to miss those kids.

"Look, a woolly mammoth!" I pointed and yelled, anticipation approaching precarious levels.

Iceberg shook his head at me. "Arjay, now even you're starting with the insults about my size? I thought you were better than that. And you know these hair implants are expensive to remove."

Harken tapped Iceberg on the shoulder and pointed him to the living, breathing woolly mammoth standing behind him in the Extinct No More section. Past the crowds vidding themselves in front of a flock of dodos in one enclosure and a black albino rhinoceros in another, was Woolly,[77] the Great American Zoo's star attraction. Woolly's curved tusks measured 10.23 feet and 10.68 feet. He was eleven feet high at the shoulder and weighed 11,857 pounds. The fee to sit on his lofty back was beyond exorbitant, which was exactly how much the 2,435 people waiting in line were willing to pay to enjoy six seconds each on the back of the world's third (and newest!) living woolly mammoth. The people waiting for their turn were mainly quiet, deep in concentration. Most were trying to decide what funny face or hand gesture they should make while sitting on Woolly

---

[77] When he was successfully synthesized, a naming contest was held for the zoo's first woolly mammoth. Children voted by the tens of thousands. *Woolly* won. Other top contenders included *Hairy, Mammothy, Tusky, Michael*, and *What's-The-Big-Deal-It's-Basically-Just-An-Elephant*.

and what hilarious comment should caption the holo-pic. The scaffolding reached right to the mammoth's back. Have no fear for those about to sit on the mighty woolly mammoth. It wasn't at all risky. Woolly was as serene and well trained as any old-timey circus elephant.[78]

I told Harken that the ring's signature was near, no more than 146 feet ahead. It drew us closer to the Mammoth Habitat, which, though quite large, was not named for its size. The low, clear fence afforded the throng of people an unimpeded view of Woolly. Iceberg easily pushed through the dense crowd to the edge of the enclosure. Harken and I followed in his wake until we all stood at the fence and were close enough to see the stitching of Woolly's saddle. "There it is."

"Where?" Harken asked.

"On the ground." I pointed at Woolly's giant front left foot.

The ring was there, on the ground, just like I said, 2.71 inches from Woolly's giant front left foot.[79] Harken saw it and detected faster than immediately that it was not attached to Nutella's finger or any other part of her. She wasn't there and neither was Pretty Lovely. Harken was befuddled. "That complicates things. Iceberg, you wanna go in there and get that ring?"

"No, Frank Harken. No, I do not."

"I'm sure it's safe. You're about as big as Woolly."

"You are so funny. I didn't see a joke about my size coming."

"I'll make a bigger one next time."

"Ha. That's me laughing at how funny you are. What do we need that ring for, anyway?"

---

[78] Which is to say that it was impossible to predict precisely when he would become enraged and trample everyone in sight.

[79] It was unfair that mammoths had feet when so many other animals had paws or hooves.

"It should tell us where Pretty Lovely is. It's synced to a tracker on her. That's how the assassin[80] found her. It's also what brought us to Win-Fall."

"What's it doing in a mammoth enclosure?"

"I don't know."[81]

"So this is a dead end?" Iceberg sounded more relieved than disappointed.

"Not if the ring still works and the tracker is still on Pretty Lovely. In that case, we just need the ring, and we'll be on our way."

"Why would the assassin leave the ring for us to find if the tracker still worked?"

"Could be a delaying tactic. Send us here to the zoo in search of the ring, leaving more time to find out what Pretty Lovely knows without us interfering."

"Could be. Or it could be a way to get us stomped to death by a woolly mammoth and off the trail for good."

While Iceberg and Harken debated the intricacies of the case and what purpose the assassin might have had for leaving the ring for us to find, and argued about what method of retrieving the ring was least likely to get everyone stomped to death, Woolly the mammoth shifted his stance. His giant front left foot came down solidly on the ring. It didn't make a sound. Or the sound was muffled by the mammoth's giant front left foot. Either way, I knew instantly that the ring had been reduced to a fine powder. Its receiving signature was gone. Just like that, our epic fellowship in quest of the ring was finished, not unlike a piece of jewelry that had been obliterated by the giant front left foot of a formerly extinct pachyderm.

---

[80] Iceberg was currently unaware of any details of Nutella's involvement, and the crafty detective had no reason to tell him more than he needed to know.

[81] The answer seemed obvious enough. The ring wasn't doing anything in the mammoth enclosure. It just sat there.

As much as I was reveling in the fun I'd had at the zoo, I couldn't help but notice that Frank Harken was not full of joy. It had been a long[82] half-day since first meeting Pretty Lovely at the food court, and it wasn't over yet. The ring was destroyed. We didn't even have a clue. I handed him a coffee to fill him up and he thanked me wordlessly.

We stood in Blue Neighborhood 290. We didn't stroll. We didn't walk. We had nowhere to go, and that's where we went, fast. There was momentary quiet. Harken had nothing to say. Iceberg had nothing to say. I, however, always had something to say, so I said it. "It looks like the trail's gone cold." According to my ongoing research about detectives and investigations, this was what to say when you didn't even have a clue.

That appeared to be quite helpful to the great detective, who looked at me and sighed.

---

[82] That's what Harken claimed. I could find no empirical evidence that this half-day was longer than any other.

I tried another one. "It's like looking for a needle in a haystack." I didn't know why someone would be doing this. It seemed to me that it would be easier and safer to buy a new needle and avoid rolling around in the hay altogether. But it meant something like, *This is hard to find because it is small and our area to search is large.* That message fit our current situation very well and, I hoped, might be just what Harken needed to figure out what to do next.

Harken looked away, shook his head. I got the message—needles and haystacks were *not* going to help us find Pretty Lovely. He was at an impasse. Six minutes and twenty-seven seconds passed with no progress of any kind. Harken stared at the floor, thinking and thinking but concluding nothing of value. My emphasizing the difficulty of our search had dampened his spirits. What he needed to hear was the opposite, that the answer was not hard to find at all.

"Frank Harken, there's probably a clue right under your nose."

He perked up.[83] "Right under my nose?"

"Right under your nose."

"What the hell's it doing there?"

"I don't know. This one confuses me, too. It's supposed to mean that it's easy to find because it's right in front of your eyes, but for some reason it isn't actually right in front of your eyes. Instead, it's right under your nose. If you think about it, that would make it incredibly difficult to find, because you can't see anything that's right under your nose, on account of your nose blocking your view. It's also unsanitary, given the number of germs lurking under the typical nose. Really, it isn't a good place for what you're looking for to be. Something right under your nose is likely to remain hidden *and* be disgusting."

Harken shot me one of his patented what-the-tarnation-is-wrong-with-you looks. "Arjay, are you malfunctioning again? Because there's a steel trashcan over there I'd be happy to throw at you if necessary."

---

[83] This might have been caused by the coffee he was drinking.

"I'm not malfunctioning."

"Are you sure? Maybe I should throw it at you just in case."

"Thank you for the generous offer. However, I am functioning at a high degree of efficiency at the moment. Don't be disappointed. Maybe there will be occasion for you to throw a trashcan at me later."

"We can hope."

"I understand your frustration. It's quite a perplexing turn of phrase. But don't blame me—I'm not the one who came up with it. I would just say *right in front of your eyes* if that's where something was. Perhaps if your nose were especially small, you might be able to see what's under it, but only if what's under it is big. Even a small nose would block a small item from view if that item were right under it. It's too bad noses don't have eyeballs. If noses had eyeballs, they'd be able to see what's right under them with no trouble at all."

"If noses had eyeballs? Arjay, seriously, that trashcan doesn't look very heavy. Your verbal program might need to be reset. If noses had eyeballs, they'd be *eyes*. Noses aren't for seeing." At that instant, a giant lightbulb didn't appear above Harken's head, because this isn't a cartoon. But he did brighten. "Arjay, that's it!"

"That's what?"

"The clue."

"What clue?"

"Arjay, you're right."

"Frank Harken, I don't know what you're referring to. I was just trying to cheer you up with some optimistic detective talk."

"Well, it worked. It's right under our noses, all right. We can't *see* it. But we might be able to *smell* it."

"Frank Harken, you're babbling...more than usual. Would it help if I threw that trashcan at you?"

"No, Arjay. No, it would not. Kind of you to ask. But it *would* help if you could bring up the schematics of this region of the Great American."

"Bring up the schematics? I'm not R2-D2."

"Who?"

The things Frank Harken didn't know! "A fictional 20th-century bot famous for being resourceful despite its deplorable communication skills and utter lack of coffee-brewing capacity. It had the schematics needed to defeat the evil Empire. I don't have schematics, but I can locate most things in the Great American. What are we looking for?"

"A bakery."

"A bakery?"

"Not just any bakery. The biggest bakery around. We're looking for cake. Delicious cake. Lots and lots of delicious cake."

Ah, the mysterious workings of a brilliant detective's mind! Somehow, he had associated nose with smell with scent with 'how-on-earth-did-Nutella-have-such-a-tasty-aroma?' It must have been because she spent so much of her time around delicious cake. It wasn't an association I would have made, but Harken was confident. To be fair, I had only been a detective for half a day, whereas Frank Harken had been a detective for a bit longer. He knew that, in the absence of any actual clues, a great detective's hunch was often good enough. Harken reasoned that Nutella had ditched the ring at the zoo on her way to a hidden base, figuring the smell of animals would throw us off her scent.

There were nine Cakewalk locations close to the Great American Zoo. The chain specialized in serving the richest, moistest, most heavenly dessert to calorie-conscious consumers who refused to compromise on cake. Each Cakewalk was an oval quarter-mile walking track encircling[84] a counter staffed by knowledgeable and friendly cakeateers. Hungry cakewalkers in four lanes burned calories with each lap (slower traffic staying to the right, of course), switching to the left lane by the counter to pick up a portion of cake when a cakeateer signaled they had earned the calories.

---

[84] *Enovaling,* if you prefer.

Iceberg was sad to learn we weren't going to a Cakewalk location, because he agreed with their marketing campaign that they had the "best cake around and around." However, he was happy to at least be part of the where-are-we-going discussion this time. Harken believed that Nutella was too thoroughly infused with cakeness for her fragrance to be retail-based. She didn't smell like that by hanging out in a Cakewalk, which dedicated most of its space to its walking track and serving area. Individual locations didn't have the square[85] footage to bake the desserts onsite. No, as tempting as a retail location smelled, the cake scent would be strongest at the source, a central bakery supplying all the local Cakewalks. Harken had deduced that only an intense concentration could be responsible for Nutella's scrumptious scent. Now he just needed to determine where the cakes were made.

Strangely, this mundane information was not a matter of public record. Why would anyone keep it secret? Harken didn't know, but he wasn't worried. It was a simple matter for me (an impossible task for anyone else) to extrapolate from the nine nearest Cakewalk locations. Based on the data and the most efficient distribution pattern, cross-referencing water and electricity usage and regional transactions of flour, baking powder, and sugar, and discarding conflicts with known establishments, I rectangulated[86] all points until I settled on the likely source of the delicious dessert. My degree of surety was a paltry 84%. Harken said that was all the surety he needed.

Beneath the shopping district was the manufacturing level of the Great American. It was always referred to as the garden level, because it was a basement. The garden level lacked the open-air layout and atrium windows of the shopping district.

---

[85] Oval footage was not as useful, apparently.

[86] Like triangulating, but more so. Everything seemed to be about shapes lately.

The garden level also lacked the festive atmosphere provided by marching accordionists and retail kiosks. What the garden level did not lack was white cinderblocks. All the walls were made up of too many of those for even me to count. (That is, of course, false, but now you know that there really were a lot of them.) Exposed pipes zigzagged along the high ceiling throughout the maze of corridors and factory space and occasionally went vertical to the floor. There weren't any flowers.

You could wander the garden level for a long time without encountering a single person. People preferred the shopping and residential levels. They could take the elevator down if they wanted, but few wanted. The garden was staffed entirely by bots. Each was designed for its assigned task. Some bots assembled, some carved, some welded, some hammered, some painted, and some did other things that needed doing, depending on what was being produced. Some bots made shoes. Some made cologne. Some made mini-golf clubs. Some made eyeliner. Some made playglobes.

Bots in the Cakewalk distribution center did things involved in making cake. Some bots hauled barrels of flour and sugar, some poured, some mixed, some whisked, some blended, some iced. Some especially lanky and swift multi-armed bots placed and removed cake pans from twenty-three-foot-tall oven towers, 124 cakes at a time per column, fifty-eight columns per row, five rows occupying the entire length of the factory. Other bots sliced and boxed cake and prepared shipments for delivery to retail locations.

We caught the scent of cake long before we had come anywhere near the bakery distribution center. Harken knew instantly he had been right to trust his hunch and said it smelled like Nutella times a million. I forgave his inexact math. As we reached the entrance, Iceberg took a deep breath and nearly fell into a sugar coma. He stayed conscious only because of the extraordinarily high tolerance he'd developed through his long and steady consumption of entire tubs of soda. Harken breathed normally and drank from the coffee I'd handed him to guard against the air's sweet effects.

We walked through the bakery factory. Like many garden facilities, it was open for touring. Production transparency was an early Great American principle and, at one time, factory tours were quite popular. People had enjoyed seeing bots at work. No one bothered coming down to the basement anymore to watch bots produce shoes and mini-golf supplies and cake. A gated path wormed through the heart of the Cakewalk production area, providing hypothetical curious humans with an intimate look at how the tasty treats were made while also preventing them from stealing product or contaminating supplies.

I knew that good manners were the linchpin of civilization, which is why I eagerly began conversing with the cakebots on the factory floor. "Hello, mixbot," I said to a dull orb with ten angled arms culminating in extendable spinning whisks. "Greetings," I called to a barrowbot rolling a thousand pounds of flour to one of thirty central mixing vats set into the floor. "How do you do?" I asked a fudgebot slicing fudge with its six fudgeblades. None of the bots replied.

"Arjay, we don't have time for social hour."

"I understand, Frank Harken. These cakebots don't seem to be in the mood for conversation, anyway." Etiquette was a lost art, but Harken was right. This wasn't the time to lecture bots about the proper way to respond to a friendly greeting. We were on a case and had to maintain our focus.

Iceberg gazed longingly at a table of cakes being iced by a team of long-armed icingbots on the other side of our gated path. Poor guy was hungry again. For a fleeting moment I wished someone would invent an affordable, loyal, competent sodabot to help him in times like this. Then I resumed not caring about it and resumed taking pride in Harken's evident enjoyment of his coffee. We had traveled along the tour path another 5.77 feet when I sensed the signal and stopped.

"What is it, Arjay?"

"It's an attempted scramble, like the one I experienced with Nutella outside Winsome Smiles[87] earlier. Someone is trying to

---

[87] The store.

render me helpless, but don't worry about it. During dinner, I reconfigured my systems to prevent such a sneaky attack from succeeding a second time."

Harken looked relieved. "I'm glad to hear that. I don't need you going on about kumquats and forklifts again. Not when we're obviously close to finding Nutella and Pretty Lovely. Very close."

The scrambling signal ceased, but I had locked in on its source. "It's coming from beneath us."

Harken was doubtful. "There is no beneath us—the garden is the lowest level of the Great American."

"It should be the lowest level, but that's where the signal's coming from."

Harken hesitated a moment and thought about it. "Arjay, your detecting has been accurate all day. I trust you. Our next move is yours to make."

We didn't yet have a matching set of monogrammed magnifying glasses, but I felt more like the famous detective's partner than ever. The next move I made was through the gate. Because it was strong, almost as solid as the bars of the GAS station holding cell, it required 22.32 seconds for me to slice through the metal spindles and roll off the path and onto the bakery production floor. Harken and Iceberg followed. Our large friend was tempted to eat cake from the icing table as we passed, but Harken shot him a look that said, *We're on a case, we don't have time for you to eat an entire table of cake.* A chastened Iceberg put down the piece of cake he was holding and continued following Harken and me as we weaved around busy cakebots and came to the floor-level mixing vat in the center of the space.

I pointed. "Down there."

The steel vat looked the same to Harken as the other twenty-nine central vats. Its rounded upper rim was only 2.67 inches above the floor, ideally heighted for barrowbots to dump a thousand pounds of sugar, flour, baking powder, eggs, chocolate chips, or whatever into the mix that made up the delicious cakes. The vat had a diameter of eight feet and was six feet deep. "You want me to go down there?"

"You are correct." He was correct.

He'd said the next move was mine, that he trusted me, and he'd meant it. He hesitated not at all before handing me his coffee and sliding into the vat. His feet touched the metal floor within. Its false bottom gave way faster than immediately. Frank Harken was gone. He'd fallen through the vat, just as I expected.

Iceberg was next. He hesitated. "What's down there?"

"I don't know." I didn't. Not exactly. Something was down there. Maybe several somethings. Possibly more.

"What if I get stuck?" He was genuinely self-conscious about his size. It was a shame, because what he really should have been self-conscious about was that bold swath of neck hair.

"You won't get stuck."

"How do you know?"

I didn't know for sure. Iceberg was quite large. But minutes counted. If he did get stuck, I had the tools necessary to get past him, though I hoped to avoid using my vibrational saw. "You'll be fine. There's a double tub of soda down there waiting for you." The opposite of hesitation ensued. Iceberg moved like a man who really, really, really[88] wanted to drink an entire double tub of soda, more than twice as fast as he would have moved for a single tub. Despite lacking the capacity for feelings or thoughts, the vat built to hold thousands of pounds of cake batter seemed relieved to have a false bottom as Iceberg slid in. He fell through with a whoosh.

I brought up the rear. More accurately, I brought it down. Way, way down—I was the last one down the rabbit hole.

---

[88] This isn't a footnote. It's the number of *reallys* you should imagine to fully appreciate how much Iceberg did not move like a glacier.

We weren't late for a very important date. Nevertheless, down we went at speeds of fifty-five miles per hour. It was just as well, since, late for a date or not, minutes counted. The enclosed slide hidden beneath the vat's false bottom dropped at an eighty-two-degree angle. Plummeting sixty-three feet was a nice touch of excitement for Harken and Iceberg. A little slow for my tastes, but fast enough to make the big man scream. Fortunately, he didn't get stuck, and mercifully the screams were not of the same pitch as screams that certainly would have accompanied even minimal use of my vibrational saw. If I had ears, that sound might have irritated them.

The slide leveled off and out I flew. Sticking the landing with my fourteen strategically positioned wheels was simplicity itself. I came to a neat stop after one graceful pirouette, still holding the coffee Harken had handed me before he'd entered the vat-slide. I hadn't spilled a drop, because I never do. Harken was waiting for me. He stood, calm and composed, looking rather dapper in his black slacks and shirt. I gave him his coffee.

Iceberg also waited, looking less dapper and not at all calm and composed. He was crumpled in a heap on the floor in the middle of the room, a well-dressed whale beached on a tiled shore, his white bowtie askew and his arching neck hair askewer. His body was not as injured as his pride, and he straightened his bowtie and the rest of himself out as he got to his feet. Iceberg was disappointed—in me and in the universe—when he saw that not even a single tub of soda waited for him. I would have felt bad about deceiving him if it were the sort of thing I could feel bad about. It wasn't.

The room was a bare square of fourteen feet by fourteen feet. There was no door, just cinderblock walls and a large circular light in the ceiling. And, protruding from one wall, the chute exit from which we'd entered, through which flowed the continuous dizzying aroma of freshly iced cake from the garden bakery above. Of course, a slide to nowhere—to a room without exits—didn't make sense. Harken said that we had entered a world of subterfuge. We should expect appearances to be deceiving. I asked him if we should also expect the unexpected. He told me that wasn't possible, but I should be ready for anything. I told him I hoped it would suffice to be ready for some things. Because that's what I was ready for.

Harken held his coffee high, catching the steady sweet breeze from the chute. The air had to be going somewhere. Steaming coffee wisped toward the wall opposite the slide. If you had the observant eyes of a great detective, perhaps you could have seen the steam diffuse through unseen gaps in the wall's corners and edges. I had no eyes, yet could see it quite clearly. The steam went there because that's where the flowing cake air went. Harken knew that's where we had to go. He examined the wall, feeling all around, found nothing.

"Arjay, this isn't a wall."

I didn't know how he reached this conclusion. By conventional standards, the wall seemed to possess an exceeding amount of wallness.

Iceberg agreed with me. "It looks like a wall."

"Exactly. That's how we know it isn't one. Remember, *subterfuge*."

Iceberg wasn't convinced by Harken's detective logic. "If it isn't a wall, what is it?"

"It's a door."

"Looks more like a wall."

"Precisely. Iceberg, you of all people should know that there can be more to something than what we see on the surface."

It was true. He *should* know. "Okay, Harken, let's say it is a door. How does it open?"

"Probably some signal or password we don't know. We'll have to force it. Come here and push on this wall."

Iceberg objected. "How many times do I have to tell you I'm more than a mere brute and that I have other interests?"

"Fifty-seven ought to be enough. You can read about the latest fashions and recite poetry later. Right now we have a wall to push. It's time to earn your dinner."

"I told you I'd pay you back for the brisket. I'm waiting for funds to clear."

"I'm sure you will." Harken pointed at the wall.

Iceberg stepped to the white cinderblocks, eclipsing them in his white tuxedo camouflage. He leaned into the wall, his legs wide for leverage and his hands high. A sugar rush of cake aroma coursed through his tremendous frame. The wall creaked. It sounded downright doorlike. Hidden gears and hinges gave a little. He pushed some more. When he seemed to be tiring, I told him there was an entire triple tub of soda waiting on the other side. He got lower and jammed his right shoulder into the wall, pushing and pushing. Gears gave a little more. We could feel air flowing past us through the 1.3821-inch crevice Iceberg's pushing had revealed at the top of the wall. Then silent gears engaged and the wall pulled away from Iceberg, lowering like a drawbridge. He stopped pushing. It lowered and lowered until it was a path into another, much larger room.

Cake wind blew us along the wall that was now the floor, a path, an entrance. We weren't alone. At the end of the path up ahead stood Nutella, her billowing mini-skirt beckoning, a lighthouse guiding lost ships in the night. And icebergs. The big man was surprised to recognize our welcoming host from his visit to Drink or Swim earlier today. "Hey, what's Hotness the bartender doing here?"

It was a warehouse. Metal shelving stacked everywhere with crates and boxes lined twelve broad aisles. There were no bots in sight. A woman in yellow work overalls operated an old-fashioned forklift,[89] the kind with tank treads and tines and articulated arms for maneuvering supplies high on the shelves. The room was cavernous. By this I mean it was literally a cavern, a natural cave formation deep in the ground that had been floored and lighted. The echo was lovely.[90]

I probably should mention that eight masked men stood behind Nutella. Their masks revealed only eyes, eyes that squinted behind eight rifles. The eight rifles aimed at us were not the kind that stunned. And they definitely were not the kind that shot coupons. That was okay because we weren't shopping. Nutella raised her left hand and spread her fingers, signaling her troops to back off. They did, their full-body fatigues melting into the cavernous shadows and fading from sight. Even I could no longer detect them.

"How delightful to see you again, Detective Harken." She still smelled great, but now so did everything. Cake breezed all around us. Nutella looked from Harken to Iceberg, back to Harken. "For someone who works alone, you've acquired quite a large entourage since this afternoon."

Iceberg took this personally. That's where he always took everything. "What do you mean, *large*? I'll have you know that there is far more to me than meets the eye."

"I'm sure there is. That tuxedo looks a couple of sizes too small."

---

[89] There was no comparing it to apples and oranges. Or kumquats.

[90] No relation to our client.

"Listen, Hotness, I didn't come here to be insulted."

"*Hotness*? Harken, you want to bring your man up to speed?"

Harken shrugged. "This is about as quick as he gets."

"I don't need both of you making fun of me." Iceberg almost shed a tear.

Nutella was taken aback. "What's your problem?"

Iceberg had worked himself into a fine tizzy. "What's my problem? I'll tell you what my problem is—"

Nutella interrupted. "—You don't have to announce that you're going to tell me. Just go ahead and tell me. It might help you get up to speed a little faster."

Iceberg's tizzy went from fine to rough. Steam didn't shoot out of his ears, but his face did turn red. "My problem? My problem is I was promised several tubs of soda that have not materialized."

"Five, to be precise," I said. I knew this because I had done the promising.

Nutella looked at Iceberg as one might look at a child crying over dropped ice cream. "That's what this is about? Will you stop complaining if I get you some soda?" Nutella snapped her fingers, and from the dull edge of darkness emerged a shrouded man with an entire tub of soda. He handed it to Iceberg and then receded, disappearing into cavernous walls. I have to say that the service here was exemplary.

With Iceberg now occupied and intensely sipping, Harken spoke to Nutella. "You have some explaining to do."

"About what?"

"About lots."

"I'm not a mind reader. You want to pick one?"

"For starters, you lied to me when you said you were a bartender."

"A pretty weak starter. That wasn't a lie. It was an incomplete truth. I tend bar. You saw me tending. Besides, you're the famous detective—you should have detected that there was more to me than meets the eye."

Harken didn't know if that was possible—Nutella met the eye with plenty already. Anyway, bartending lies were only the beginning. "And you stole my ring and then sent me on a wild goose[91] chase to the zoo."

"Yes," she acknowledged. "Did you enjoy your visit?"

He didn't answer, so I said, "I did." It's true. I had.

Harken wasn't through listing grievances. "And you used me to distract Tommy Ten-Toes so you could take Pretty Lovely."

Nutella laughed. "Yes, I did. Brilliant, wasn't it?"

"And you messed with Arjay."

"What's an arjay?"

I said, "I am." It's true. I was.

"You know this is Arjay,[92] my coffeemaker. You scrambled his verbal program when you stole the ring. I had to smash him with a trashcan to fix it."

"Subtle. Remind me not to ask you for tech support."

"Nutella, I'm on a case. I don't appreciate you interfering with my investigation."

She laughed. "You call what you've been doing *investigating*? How cute. I can hardly keep myself from pinching your cheeks. Detective, you don't know the first thing about this case."

"I know lots of first things about this case. It's the second things I can't seem to figure out. None of it makes any sense."

"Harken, you want things to make sense, you're in the wrong line of work. Also, the wrong universe."

---

[91] I neglected to mention the geese we saw at the Great American Zoo. They pooped everywhere, which has always been a wild goose's primary vocation. This was true for the domesticated ones as well. Goose poop was among the world's most plentiful renewable resources.

[92] I had introduced myself to Nutella earlier outside Pretty Lovely's housing unit. I attributed her poor memory to her incomprehensible dislike of coffee.

"Maybe you're right. One thing I'm having trouble making sense of is *you*. What's your angle?[93] What is this place?"

"Wouldn't you like to know?"

"Yes, I would. That's why I asked."

Nutella smiled a natural smile that said, *Okay, I'll tell you, but only because of how cute you are and how I can hardly keep myself from pinching your cheeks.* "Detective, you've stumbled onto a base of a secret organization. I'm with the Great American Defense."

"Never heard of it."

"That's what makes it a secret."

"That's what *made* it a secret. I've heard of it now. No more deception. If we're gonna be working together, you'd better bring me up to speed."

"Not so fast. Who said we're working together? Maybe I work alone." She was enjoying herself.

"You came to me at Diamond Row and asked what *our* next move was. I now accept your offer."

"That wasn't a genuine offer. I knew you'd decline. I just wanted the ring."

Harken smiled a natural smile of his own. "Enough with the games. You need me."

"I need *you*? What do I need you for? I have Pretty Lovely. I have GAD's resources. What do you have? Your promiscuous reputation as a great detective?"

"That. And maybe something else." He looked at me.

Nutella looked at me.

Even Iceberg looked at me, between sips of what was left of an entire tub of soda.

Nutella thought about it. "The coffee's that good?"

Harken nodded. "You know that it is."

It's true. Despite her inability to remember names and her dislike of coffee, she did.

---

[93] Ninety degrees. She had excellent posture.

We entered a tunnel of carved-out rock at the rear of the warehouse and navigated through a maze of lefts and rights and rights and lefts while Nutella brought us up to speed. The Great American Defense wasn't commonly known as GAD because it wasn't commonly known at all, on account of it being a secret organization. However, those in the know knew that's what it was called. We weren't yet completely in the know, but we were no longer completely in the know-not, either, so we could call it GAD if we wanted to. Though, since we must never mention it to anyone and would certainly be obliterated if we did, we really had no need to call it anything.

GAD was everywhere and nowhere. You might say it was clandestine if you were foolish enough to say anything at all. It was best to keep the whole thing on the QT if you could fit it there. Any extra should be kept on the down-low. GAD might have been a riddle, wrapped in a mystery, inside an enigma, though it's possible that was a disguise. Nevertheless, it was pretty hard to explain. Nutella would tell us more about it, but then she'd have to kill us. She knew this sounded like the punch line to a tired old joke. It wasn't. She never joked about killing. Okay, sometimes she did. But she wasn't this time. We had to remember that loose lips sink ships. It didn't matter that GAD had no ships. What mattered was that the ships GAD didn't have stayed unsunk.

Who could argue with that? Not Harken. He was too busy trying to figure out what she was talking about. It wasn't easy processing such a substantial quantity of non-information. And not Iceberg. He didn't know what Hotness the bartender was talking about, either. He thought perhaps the reference to sinking ships was a jab at his size and name and was waiting for her to take a breath so he could express his deep disappointment that she didn't realize there was more to him than met the eye. Iceberg never got the chance.

When that breath came, it was furtive and quick, like Nutella herself. She went right on talking. There was much she couldn't tell us. What she could tell us is that GAD was the last line of defense. Or was it the first? Possibly the middle. It was a line of defense, that much was certain. Against what? The Great American had enemies, that's what. All great civilizations did (lamentably, mini-golf envy was a universal human trait). Even mediocre civilizations had enemies, though of course the great ones had many more.[94] GAD was sworn to oppose them. Nutella was proud to help protect the greatest civilization of all. That's what had brought her to Drink or Swim.

She had been embedded as a bartender for nearly five months, deep undercover in a bikini as Hotness. Her assignment was to get to know fellow bartender Winsome Smiles. Reliable and unreliable sources had linked Winsome to the Destroyers, a group of ne'er-do-wells known for never doing well, among other things. Punks like that were usually beneath notice if not contempt, and only came to GAD's attention because of unusual levels of chatter intercepted from the outside. Something bigger than broken retail displays was in the works. Nobody knew what. Nutella said Winsome was a peripheral player at best. She was GAD's way in—that was all. Nutella had worked for months to win her trust, work that finally began to pay off two nights ago when Winsome promised to introduce Hotness to some friends—the Destroyers. Then Winsome disconnected.

"And?" Harken asked.

"And what?" Nutella asked right back.

"Sounds to me like you might know the first thing about this case, but what about the second and third? You and GAD's mighty resources are as in the dark as I am. You were undercover for five months? At least I managed to know next to nothing in less than a day."

"Intelligence work requires patience, Harken. I was about to infiltrate the group, would have done so any day now if Winsome hadn't disconnected and gone missing. We only knew she was missing for sure when Pretty Lovely disconnected as well. That was today."

---

[94] That's how we knew they were great. It was the second surest indication, right after mini-golf.

"I know it was today. I was there when you found out. Speaking of Pretty Lovely, she's *my* client. I need to speak with her."

"We've tried that already. She doesn't know anything."

"Doesn't know, or won't say?"

"Doesn't know. We can be very persuasive."

"Did you hurt her?"

"Don't get your adorable feathers ruffled, Harken. Your client is fine."

Frank Harken didn't have feathers. If he did, they would be smooth. A little tickly, perhaps, but definitely not adorably ruffled. He just needed to speak to his client. Nutella had no problem with that. We were heading that way already and would be there in a minute.

Iceberg had been silent during our walk through the tunnel. Now, as we exited, he weighed in on the case with the kind of perception Harken had come to expect from the man who had a lot more to him than meets the eye. "Excuse me, Hotness, but before we talk to Pretty Lovely, could we stop at a bathroom?" Iceberg had consumed an entire tub of soda and, from the tone of his voice and his constant shifting from one foot to the other, it was clear to everyone that the matter was rather urgent.

Minutes counted, but don't tell Iceberg that. He exited the bathroom and was instantly offended by Harken's impatiently crossed arms. Didn't the detective know it wasn't healthy to hold in an entire tub of soda? Not to mention a heaping plate of brisket? Harken wished Iceberg hadn't mentioned it—maybe the big guy could try to have a little more decorum than spider monkeys and bears in the woods and wild geese. Some things were best kept private. Iceberg didn't understand why Harken was squeamish. It was a natural process. Everyone did it. They were mammals after all, just like the monkeys, bears, and geese.[95]

I was pleased to not be an everyone. Or a mammal. Specifically, I was glad not to spend so much time thinking about food and talking about food, and so much time eating food, only to evacuate the results in such undignified fashion. Besides, I could see no benefit to having hair and nipples. Harken thanked

---

[95] Geese weren't mammals any more than white was slimming—large as he was, Iceberg wasn't big on facts.

me for my edifying contribution to the conversation. On behalf of mammals everywhere, my opinions were noted and appreciated. I didn't think Harken had the authority to speak for mammals everywhere. There were too many constituencies for him to possibly represent anything more than an infinitesimal fraction. I calculated that 0.000000017% was a generous maximum.

Nutella said one mystery was solved, anyway. It was clear now why we didn't know the first thing about this case. Maybe some of our energy should be focused on solving it instead of this incessant meaningless prattle. I told her I didn't know what other kind of prattle existed, but I was eager to learn. Nutella wanted to know if I had any idea how exasperating I was. I said I had *some* idea. Would that suffice? She asked Harken how he put up with me. His answer was I made exceptional coffee. However, he was more than happy[96] to change the subject and focus on the case. They talked while we made our way through a series of corridors deeper underground.

"Nutella, you worked with Winsome for five months. What do you think happened to her?"

"I don't know."

"I know you don't *know*. That's why I asked you what you *think*."

"Harken, you're the detective. What do *you* think happened to her?"

He shrugged. "We don't have a lot to go on. Winsome stopped showing up for work a day ago and she disconnected even though she never disconnects. She's somehow involved with the Destroyers, doesn't get along with her father, is being shadowed by GAD, and Tommy Ten-Toes wants to find her so bad, he abducted her sister Pretty Lovely and sent Iceberg with me. Anything else?"

"That's about it."

---

[96] He didn't specify how much more. Probably forty-seven. That was a popular number.

"Doesn't narrow things down much. Could be she was kidnapped. Could be she owes someone money and is in hiding. Could be she crossed the wrong person and is dead. Could be she's fine and this is a grab for attention. Could be something else altogether and she's gotten in over her head."[97]

"Could be all sorts of things," Nutella agreed. "Let's hope she's not dead. She's important to me."

"Nice to know you care."

"I do care. I've spent five months building trust so I could infiltrate the Destroyers. If she got herself killed, I'm gonna have to start over. Except I doubt there's even time for that. Chatter indicates something's going down soon."

"Touching. Don't worry. She's probably alive. If she wasn't conscious when she disconnected, a rescue squad would have been automatically dispatched. At the least, Winsome was alive then."

Nutella nodded. "True. So why would she disconnect?"

"Maybe someone forced her to. Could be the same someone keeping her off the peacegrid and keeping GAS out of this."

"Could be. The Destroyers routinely evade the peacegrid and block surveillance. It's a major escalation in their capabilities from a year ago, part of what got our attention in the first place. Tech like that isn't easy to find."

The corridor opened into a wider room with lockers along a wall. The eight masked, camouflaged men who'd politely greeted us with their rifles earlier were now around a table, playing poker. The masks must have made it tough to tell when one of them was bluffing. The space narrowed into a corridor again, and we continued walking.

"Where's the tech coming from?" Harken asked.

"We don't know," Nutella said.

"Is it possible Winsome figured out who you were? Maybe she disconnected and disappeared to get away from GAD."

---

[97] I wasn't a full-fledged detective yet, but this last one seemed unlikely to me. As a bartender at Drink or Swim, Winsome would have to be a strong swimmer.

"No. She didn't see through my cover."

"You sure?"

"She had no reason to hide from me. I told you, she's just a way in. We're not interested in Winsome. Anyway, yes, I'm sure."

"Okay, you're sure. Maybe she knew Ten-Toes was looking for her and disconnected to hide from him. Iceberg, what does Tommy Ten-Toes want with Winsome?"

Iceberg was only half paying attention. The other half of his attention was focused on the difficult task of catching his breath while walking through these endless corridors. "Huh? Oh, Ten-Toes? I don't know what he wants. He doesn't tell me much."

"Shocking. I thought you were the brains behind that whole operation, what with how much more there is to you than we see on the surface. You didn't hear what he asked Pretty Lovely?"

"No. They had a quiet, private conversation over a glass of wine. All I know is she didn't tell him anything helpful and I'm supposed to stick with you till we find Winsome, then contact him."

"Oh, joy," Harken said.

"Harken," Nutella asked, "why haven't you ditched this glacier?"

"I can't do that. He's providing most of what little amusement this case has to offer."

"If you say so."

"I do. And it's easier to keep all the loose ends together. I don't know what Ten-Toes wants, but it's part of the case. I prefer to have Iceberg where I can see him."

"You can see him from orbit."

"Hey!" Iceberg had detected a joke about his size.

Nutella ignored his protest. "And what's the deal with the coffeemaker?"

"His name is Arjay."

"I haven't seen one quite like it before."

Harken agreed. "Neither have I. He showed up today... unexpectedly."

I set the record straight because no one likes a crooked one. "Ahem, Frank Harken. We already agreed that you ordered me."

"Yes, Arjay. We did agree. It must have slipped my mind."

I handed him a coffee to give his memory better traction.

He accepted it and turned back to Nutella. "At first I thought it was a shipping error."

Nutella looked at me the way a lactose-intolerant vegan might look at a bacon-wrapped steak in heavy cream. "I guess it could be a coincidence."

"Could be. I'm not a big believer in coincidences, though if there's any connection to the case, I'm not seeing it. None of this adds up to anything."

I expressed my sincere sympathy. "Math can be quite frustrating for mammals. It's even harder for insects, though. You'd think so many legs would help with counting, but you'd be wrong. Their distinct lack of fingers is a real obstacle. It's why primates are better with numbers than cows are."

"Arjay, thank you for your insightful perspective. As usual, you've given us plenty to think about."

He was right. I had.

Frank Harken asked Iceberg and Nutella to stay out in the hall while he spoke to Pretty Lovely, detective-client confidentiality being essential. We entered the lounge through the steel door. Yes, the lounge. What, did you think Nutella had Pretty Lovely holed up in a cell? Or worse, holed up in a hole? The lounge had plush carpets and dimmable lights and luxurious sofas and was filled with soft music, something by Mozart featuring violins and waterfalls. Pretty rested comfortably three feet above the sofa, hovering booster pillows supporting her head, back, and legs. Relaxing on a bed of air was very relaxing.

"Ms. Lovely, we need to talk." Harken and I stood just inside the room, with the door closed behind us.

"One moment, please, detective." She had reconnected and was in mid-chat with some distant friends through RET.[98] They were at a dance club three regions over and wanted Pretty to meet them. They hadn't seen her longer legs in person yet and thought she should show them off by dancing with them late into the night. Pretty said she had to decline because of personal reasons, which was a difficult concept for them to understand, nothing ever having been too personal for Pretty to share until now. Would she consider showing up after her personal reasons were taken care of? If she didn't have time tonight, would she meet them for third dessert in the morning when they were done dancing? Pretty promised to try.

With her silent conversation finished, she gestured for the booster pillows to lower her. As she descended, there was time to check her makeup and adjust her legstensions for the elegant seated position she assumed upon reaching the sofa. Pretty Lovely looked none the worse for wear despite her challenging day—her winter boots, long coat, and mini-skirt were in fine shape. She doubted very much that Frank Harken could even begin to imagine what she'd been through.

After discovering her sister was missing, she'd first met with the detective at 13:07. Just a little while later, she'd endured the frigid environs of Lettuce Snow, and witnessed Harken being stunned by GAS before she left with Iceberg. Following that, she met Tommy Ten-Toes. He was hospitable enough, though he had many questions and she had no answers, which made for awkward pauses and uncomfortable silences. Also, for some reason it hurt her eyes to look directly at him. Then, she saw Hotness's fierce battle with four guards and was unceremoniously transported here in some kind of secret silent sonic shuttle that had almost mussed her dazzling hair. Next, to add insult to non-injury, she was subjected to even more questions she couldn't answer. Hotness had brought her to this lounge and softened her up with wine and cheese to try to get information about the Destroyers and Winsome's whereabouts.

---

[98] Rapid Eye Text.

Pretty couldn't wait for this long day to end. "It sure hasn't been a picnic," she said.

Harken understood. "It hasn't exactly been a day at the beach for me, either."

Pretty Lovely's purple eyes turned thoughtful.[99] "Have you ever been?"

"Have I ever been what?"

"To the beach."

"Sure."

"I mean a real one, outside, on a coast?"

"Yes, I've been to a real outside beach. Back east."

"Wow. Of course, I've only gone to the ones inside. What's it like?" Her hair changed colors, blinking a pattern of tropical water and sandy beach.

Harken said, "It's been so many years. I'm sure it's different now. A lot has happened since then, you know."

"But when you went, what was it like?"

"Well, we would get up early—"

"—We?"

"My family. I was a kid. We'd get up early and load the car."

"Load the car? With what?"

"We would pack lunches, snacks, towels, and load the car with folding beach chairs, sand shovels and buckets—"

"—Didn't the beach have shovels and buckets already?"

"No. We had to bring it with us."

"That doesn't sound very convenient. There wasn't even a button to press that summoned shovels and buckets? At the Great American Beach all you do is ask for a shovel and bucket and they pop up from beneath the sand."

Harken was getting annoyed. "I know about the Great American Beach. Do you want to hear about a real one or not?"

"I'm sorry. Please, continue."

"Then we'd get in the car and wait because my mother always had to check that we hadn't forgotten sunscreen."

"Sunscreen?"

---

[99] Thoughtful is similar to orange (the color, not the fruit).

"Yes, as soon as we got to the beach we'd lather up our bodies with lotion to keep from getting sunburned."

"Detective Harken, please be serious."

"I am being serious."

She was skeptical.

Harken insisted. "Really, the sun could burn your skin."

"Fine," she said. "The sun could burn your skin. What else?"

"After we'd loaded the car, we'd drive to the beach."

"Sounds terribly dangerous, zooming around loose in those big metal caskets. Did you often crash into other cars?"[100]

"No, we didn't often crash into other cars. Driving out there wasn't as hard as people in here think it was. Plus, usually we wouldn't exactly be zooming around. Mostly we'd sit in traffic for about an hour, barely moving, with thousands of other cars also going to the beach."

"Why didn't you just go faster?"

"Because the cars in front of us were going slow."

"Why didn't they just go faster?"

"Because the cars in front of them were going slow."

"What about the cars at the very front? Why didn't they just go faster?"

"No one knows. Maybe it's similar to how there's always a crowd blocking your way when you're walking in the Great American."

She shook her head. "You can usually shuttle past that if you have somewhere to be. There wasn't a shuttle to the beach?"

"No, there wasn't a shuttle. You had to drive there and then drive around for twenty minutes looking for a place to park. Sometimes we'd find a close spot. Other times not so close. Sometimes we'd give up and pay for a parking spot."

"Cars sound like a lot of work."

---

[100] Self-driving cars had reduced accidents by 87.3% until one Thanksgiving weekend when a talented hacker trying to win a bet caused 23,956 fatalities, after which humans insisted on driving their own cars again and accidents became more common.

"I guess. After parking, we'd all grab some stuff. Beach chairs, sand toys, cooler, umbrella—"

"Umbrella? Why did you go to the beach in the rain? I know beaches were open-air out there, but I figured people went when it wasn't raining."

"We didn't go to the beach in the rain. The umbrella was to shade us from the sun. It was big and went into the sand and covered our chairs."

"Sunscreen? Umbrellas? How often did people melt out there?"

Harken laughed. "People didn't melt. It's just that the sun is stronger than you can tell from in here. You know the greenhouse attraction in Violet Neighborhood 246? Like that, but without filters. As I was saying, after we parked, we'd all grab some stuff and carry it to the beach. Then we'd pay and go set up our chairs and umbrellas. If we were lucky, we'd be close to the water."

"Lucky?"

"Yes. It was as crowded at the beach as it is at Lettuce Snow. Usually we'd set our things up a few hundred yards from the water."

"Odd. Then what?"

"Then we'd run as fast as we could to the ocean because the sand burned our feet. Some places, you weren't allowed to swim because of trash in the water—occasionally a hypodermic needle would float by. That wasn't usually a problem where we went, except one summer. Most other times the biggest danger was scraping our feet on broken shells hidden beneath the waves. Also, you had to watch for jellyfish. And riptides could make swimming dangerous."

"Riptides?"

"Yes. Currents could pull you out to sea, but people didn't usually drown. The lifeguards were pretty good."

"Lifeguards?"

"Yes. They were swimmers trained to pull people out of the water."

"The Great American Beach doesn't need lifeguards. It has bartenders."

"Most outside beaches didn't allow alcohol."

This genuinely surprised her. "Going to the beach must have been terrifying."

"Not usually. Sharks weren't very common. There were only a few attacks each year."

"People brought their children to these places?"

"All the time."

"Parents really were crazy on the outside. What did you do at the beach when you weren't being eaten by sharks and drowned by riptides?"

"We'd play in the water, throw a ball around, make a sandcastle. We'd eat lunch and try not to swallow too much sand. And you had to be aware of the seagulls. If you turned your back for a second, they'd swoop in and steal your food. After lunch we'd play some more until everyone was tired and then we'd pack up and go home. We'd try to get the sand off the stuff before we put it back in the car, but that never worked. You'd have sand in the car's crevices as long as you owned it no matter how much you vacuumed, though you could get the sand out of your personal crevices with a couple of showers if the water pressure was high enough. And no matter how much sunscreen you used, you always missed a spot, and you'd have a little sunburn. Did I mention you might have another hour of traffic on the way home?"

There was a mesmerizing display of blinking hair as Pretty Lovely shook her head. "Not until now. Every bit of it sounds truly awful. All that work and hassle and danger. Just horrible."

Harken was feeling nostalgic. "Actually, it was wonderful."

"I don't understand why anyone would still live outside."

"Many don't have a choice—there's a long wait to get in here. The Great American only admits people as fast as the pace of housing construction allows. And others...when you've lived out there, under an open sky, it isn't so easy to give it up. People like going to a real beach."

"Well, I'm happy I don't have to do it. The whole thing sounds like bad post-apocalyptic fiction. Packing lunch and carrying it with you? It's all so primitive. I prefer the beaches here. Thirty-minute sessions by appointment. Private. Nonstick sand. No sunburn."

"Yes, molk do seem to like it."

She corrected him. "*Meople*."

"Right, *meople*. I didn't get the memo."

"What's a memo?"

"Never mind. Enough about the beach. Let's talk about the case."

"If we must."

"We must."

Her blinking hair shifted from beach theme to primary colors. "I told Mr. Ten-Toes and Hotness—I mean Nutella— everything I know about Winsome, which lately isn't much. Despite connecting with her every day, I'm sad to say I don't know my sister very well anymore."

"I don't want to talk about your sister."

"You don't?"

"I don't. I want to talk about you."

"Me?"

"Let's start with why you lied to me."

"I'm sure I don't know what you're referring to."

"Are you sure?"

"I just said I was."

"Why'd you tell me you reported your sister missing to GAS before you came to me? I know you didn't. Why lie about that?"

"Oh. That. Does that count as a lie? I was afraid you'd tell me to go to GAS and wouldn't take the case. It was easier to tell you I'd already spoken to them."

"Why didn't you go to GAS in the first place?"

"I knew I couldn't trust them."

"How'd you know that?"

"Winsome said not to. GAS has it in for her and her friends. You were the only one I should trust."

"Winsome said that?"

Pretty nodded. Their father had regaled Winsome and Pretty with stories of Detective Frank Harken's big cases. The Beguiling Mystery of the Missing Necklace. The Unexpected Incident of the Heirloom Tomato. The Strange Times Those Three Other Things Happened That No One Else Could Figure Out. "Winsome knew you could be trusted. She said to get you if anything happened to her."

"When did she say that?"

"Last week."

"Just last week? Just last week she specifically told you to get *me* if anything happened? Why didn't you tell me this when you hired me?"

"I told you I'd never hired a private detective before. I didn't think it was important. Should I have mentioned it? —Excuse me a moment."

Harken's reply included the words *damn* and *molk* and *hell* and several others I shall not repeat because I'm not that kind of coffeemaker. Pretty Lovely didn't hear any of them. She was receiving a message. A startling, frightening message. If it were possible for her to turn paler than she already was, she might have been described as looking like a ghost. Instead, she looked like she'd seen one. Harken recognized something was wrong and stopped shouting colorful language. "What is it?"

Pretty was shaken. Also, she was shaking. Her words came out in spurts between frantic breaths. "Detective Harken, Winsome's in trouble. I mean, serious trouble. She might even be in grave danger. We're going to need money. A great deal of money. Or..."

"Or what?"

Pretty held back tears. "Or they're going to kill my sister."

The secret silent sonic shuttle was the only way to travel. Unless you counted walking. And magnetic rail. And local shuttle. And tram. And horizontal lift. And the twenty-one other ways there were to travel in the Great American. But no matter how many of them you counted, the secret silent sonic shuttle was by far the fastest. It might have been best described as a superhighway made up of a series of tubes, except it was best not described at all, on account of how secret it was. It might have been worst described as a massively larger-scale pneumatic transport like those used by ancient banks, back when money was kept in buildings and people would drive up to the bank in cars and beg a teller to send them cash[101] in a little capsule. Whether best or worst described or not described, we entered through a hidden hatch in the wall next to the lounge door—there always seemed to be a hidden hatch within Nutella's reach. GAD continued to impress Harken with its seeming-to-be-nowhere-yet-being-everywhere-ness.

---

[101] Composed of paper!

Seconds later, we exited through a hatch behind a stage in Taupe Neighborhood 315, at the concert polygon. It was a Day of Joining music festival. Simultaneous performances were being performed on nineteen stages, each stage adjacent to the next and angled to face the same center. Inside the enneadecagon[102] were 8,387 people. They sat in rotating elevator chairs that allowed them to see whichever stage they chose. To Harken, it sounded like nineteen songs being played at the same time, a cacophonic blast that made his head hurt. I handed him a coffee to protect his auditory receptors.

Connected audience members could manipulate the incoming clash, filtering out songs they didn't like and mashing up songs they did, adding sound effects they preferred. In this way, each concertgoer heard and created a unique, customized performance. Audience members could also watch and listen to the concert through the vantage point of other connected audience members (up to twelve at a time) and splice sound and vids from these different angles to create completely original songs. Few paid attention to any one musical act. The real fun of the festival was seeing what you could do with the material provided and whose mash-up would be most popular. The best ones could catch on with connected molk not in attendance, and might even propel the mash-up artist to stardom and a lucrative career as an award-winning musician. Great American talent was widely distributed.

We skirted the edge of the concert, and the humans kept their heads down to avoid attracting attention from dozens of patrolling GAS officers. Officer Gunner Claymore's restful nap had certainly ended by now, and Harken imagined he wasn't too pleased with us. We didn't believe Claymore knew where we were or that the patrols had anything to do with us—a heavy security presence was standard at music festivals. Still, we had to be cautious. Staying off the peacegrid was crucial to our investigation continuing unimpeded. Fortunately, GAS didn't

---

[102] Most people don't know that a polygon with 19 sides is common enough to have its own word.

notice us, as the officers were busy cordoning off one thing and another. The most highly trained men and women in neon yellow and red uniforms went this way and that, so we went the other.

After passing five mini-golf courses (world wars, pirates, donuts, aliens, pirates), each with a multitude waiting to play, we came to the celebrated digestive system course. A tremendous scale-facsimile of a human head, torso, and buttocks towered the height of three levels of the Great American. The crowd crowding the escalator was at least double-throng thick. Or more. Golfers escalated and then entered the course through an eight-foot-high open mouth and played the first hole past the teeth and over the tongue. The design was genuinely authentic to the last physiological detail. Activated saliva glands frequently drenched players, especially if they were tasty. Further on and lower down, it took guts to putt around stomach acid hazards and intestinal blockage. A wrong step could ruin your shoes. So could a right step.

As we passed, Iceberg pointed to a group of players squeezing through the course's final hole and said, in a tone rich with vindication, that it was a natural process and Harken had nothing at all to be squeamish about.

Harken didn't respond—he was holding his breath because, as everyone within 28.3 feet would agree, the stench at the eighteenth hole exceeded the Great American's maximum permissible malodor threshold by 516%.

Frank Harken and Nutella walked ahead of Pretty Lovely and Iceberg.

Nutella wasn't convinced we were dealing with a straightforward kidnapping. "You really think it's a simple case of ransom?"

Harken was noncommittal as he dispensed detectively wisdom. "Ransom cases are rarely simple. The simple ones least of all."

"I don't know what that means."

"Neither do I," he said. "That's how complicated ransom cases can be. But Winsome certainly appears to have been kidnapped."

Nutella dispensed some wisdom of her own. "Appearances can be deceiving, but so can disappearances."

Harken nodded. "True. Of course, everything can be deceiving. Especially deception."

Nutella agreed. "That, most of all. So what's your plan?"

"We still don't have much to go on. I plan to meet the ransomer's demands."

"Isn't that what the ransomer wants?"

"I don't know what the ransomer wants. I only know what the ransomer demanded. Three items in exchange for Winsome Smiles."

"So your plan is to let the ransomer win?"

"I'm not playing a game. My plan is to get Winsome Smiles back safely. That's what I was hired to do."

"Harken, you know there's something bigger going on here. I aim to find out what it is."

"It's a good aim. I wouldn't mind making sense of this whole thing, either, but in the meantime, I plan to keep Winsome Smiles alive. The threats to her safety were explicit. And Lovely doesn't know the ransomer. The signal was anonymous, untraceable. We'll have to see this through to the end."

At that moment, as they turned the corner, three women jumped out from the entrance of Pedicure Patio and shouted, "Surprise!" [103] The little their mini-skirts left to the imagination didn't require even a little imagination. Their heels had heels. Their eyelashes curled up to touch their foreheads. Their blouses were flattering[104] form-fitters, one of them red, one white, and one blue, appropriately festive colors for the Day of

---

[103] At the last possible instant, Nutella realized they weren't a threat. They would never know just how close she had come to roundhousing their heads in.

[104] They complimented their wearers randomly and often.

Joining. The women shouted, "Surprise!" seven more times, slurring only six of them. Yet, imperfect as their speaking capabilities were at the moment, they had a lot to say.

Pretty Lovely's friends weren't going to let "personal reasons" keep them from celebrating her new legstensions. After connecting with her and downing their drinks, and having one more round for the trip, they had left the dance club and shuttled over to see her. Had they scared her just now when they jumped out? She should see the look on her face! If she didn't want them to come, she shouldn't have connected them her location. Wow! Look at those legs! The new models were really subtle. And who was this delicious giant man in a fine white tuxedo walking next to her? A new boyfriend? Is that why Pretty got the extra-long legstensions? Because her new boyfriend was enormous and she wanted to try to see him eye to eye? In that case, gorgeous as her legstensions were, she was gonna need a longer set. He still towered over her. That was one giant hunk of man! He had beautiful arctic eyes! Oh, look, he was blushing!

Harken stopped their chitchat before it gained unstoppable momentum that might derail the entire investigation. "We don't have time for this. Minutes count."

The woman in the red blouse was the most[105] inebriated, so naturally she spoke up for the group. "Don't have time for this? Hogwash! Hooey! This is the Great American. There's time for everything! Pretty, I like your hairy boyfriend, but who is *this* Neanderthal?"

"Excuse me," I said. "You are obviously confusing your species. You might want to consider upgrading your visual apparatus. Frank Harken is far too handsome to be mistaken for a Neander—"

Harken interrupted "—Arjay, we don't have time to be arguing with molk about nonsense."

---

[105] That is, the most out of the three friends talking to Pretty Lovely, not out of *everyone* in the entire Great American. At that moment, her GAIR (Great American Inebriation Ranking) was 1,873,980.

Pretty Lovely was mortified. She apologized profusely to her friends for Harken's insensitive word choice. "I'm so sorry. My friend here—well, he's not exactly my friend—anyway, he has no couth. He doesn't follow the latest polls. I keep telling him it's *meople*."

"Oh, Pretty," the soused red-bloused woman said, laughing at her friend's ignorance, "it isn't *meople*. That's almost as offensive as molk."

Pretty was confused. "When did it stop being *meople*?"

"Forty-four minutes ago. There was a vote. Our demographic prefers to be known as *mersons*."

"See what happens when I disconnect for a couple of hours? I miss all the important news!" She turned to Harken. "It isn't *meople* any longer. Now it's *mersons*."

"I heard. I'm standing right here. Could we get on with the case?"

Pretty remembered that her sister was missing and under explicit threat from a ransomer, and politely sent her friends back to their night of partying. "Ladies, it has been a spectacular pleasure to see you. I do have to take care of something. You should get your dance on and I'll try to meet you for third dessert."

The ladies made Pretty pinky-promise to meet them for third dessert, exchanged hugs and cheek kisses and more hugs, and then rushed to catch the shuttle coming in one level above so they could resume getting their dance on.

Harken shook his head and muttered something about crazy molk driving him crazy.

Pretty Lovely had finally had too much of his hate, and sharply rebuked him. "For the last time, Detective Harken, it isn't *molk*. It's *mersons*!"

Jonathan Smiles was overjoyed to see his daughter. They embraced outside Winsome Smiles[106] and he thanked Frank Harken for his exceptionally efficient detective work. Smiles glanced at Nutella and Iceberg, but was too concerned with recent disturbing information to concern himself with asking about our group's new acquisitions. "Detective, what's this Pretty tells me about a ransom? How much do they want for my other little girl?"

"Thirty-thousand."

"Dollars?"

Nutella laughed first. It was a cross between a giggle and a chuckle. It was apparently infectious, because Harken laughed second, a cross between a chuckle and a snicker. Iceberg laughed third, a cross between a snicker and a snort. Pretty laughed fourth, a cross between a snort and a chortle. Jonathan Smiles laughed fifth, and last, his chortle rapidly becoming a guffaw, then a roaring howl. His tears flowed freely. He wiped them from his face with the back of his hands.

As Mr. Smiles regained his composure, he said, "I guess that's just wishful thinking. It feels good to laugh, though. These last few hours have been very difficult."

Harken understood. "I understand, Mr. Smiles. I wish it were dollars. That would make it easier."

Mr. Smiles was somber again. "Yes, it would. But of course it isn't. What would anyone buy with that?"

"Nothing, and not much of it. We need 30,000 of actual money."

"Where am I supposed to get 30,000?"

"You own a thriving business, Mr. Smiles. Don't you have it?"

"No. I don't have close to that, not liquid."

"Can't you get someone to loan you the money?"

"Thirty-thousand?"

"I know. It's a lot."

"Detective Harken, 30,000 is way more than a lot."

---

[106] The store.

"I know."

"I mean, 10,000 is a lot. If you said you had a lot of money, I would guess around 10,000. But 30,000? That's more."[107]

"Maybe we could use some of your inventory. Certified gemstones should be acceptable to any reputable ransomer."

"My inventory? Detective, that inventory isn't mine to use. Until I make the sale, every last item sold in my store is the property of the manufacturer's distributor. We make a bit on markup, of course, but most of our profit is on the installation. I have dozens of employees, overhead, advertising costs. You think it's easy running a business like this, that I'm swimming in money?"

"Mr. Smiles, they said they're going to kill your daughter. I'm just trying to stop that."

"How do we know they won't kill her anyway, after you've given them what they want?"

"We don't know for sure. I'll do everything I can to prevent it. You're just going to have to trust me."

Mr. Smiles didn't respond.

Pretty clasped one of her father's hands. "Daddy, please. She's my sister. She's Winsome."

Mr. Smiles looked at his no-longer-missing daughter and thought about it for a moment. "Detective Harken, you know I respect how your reputation precedes you. And I love my daughter—*both* my daughters—despite our differences. Don't doubt that for a second. I really would do anything—almost anything—to help her, to help either one of them." He was quiet another moment and reassured Pretty with a fatherly pat on her hand. "Now that I think about it, I do have some gems we could use. High quality. A total value of about 30,000 all together."[108]

"That's convenient," Harken said.

"You and I don't agree on what *convenient* means." Jonathan Smiles smiled wide, showing thirty-two diamond-encrusted teeth.

---

[107] Five times more if you're bad at math.

[108] What they totaled separately is anyone's guess. Probably not as much.

You might think removing diamonds from teeth is easy. That could be because you are wrong. The whole point of cementing gems to teeth was to keep them from being removed. Biting and chewing, meal after meal, plus snacks between meals, plus snacks between snacks, day after day and month after month,[109] could wear down any but the strongest adhesive. This could lead to swallowed diamonds. And retrieving swallowed diamonds was even less fun than it sounds.

Aside from not wanting to retrieve swallowed diamonds, customers needed extra-secure attachments because gem thieves were a real threat. Have a little too much fun getting your drink on at your shady friend's third cousin's birthday party? Fall asleep on the sofa with your mouth open? You'd better hope your mouth enhancer hadn't cheaped out on the adhesive. Many a hungover yet happy molk had become less happy by waking up to teeth that had been ungemmed in the night.

Jonathan Smiles was pleased to say that his customers had no such worries. Winsome Smiles[110] used only premium cement and a nine-step process that flawlessly bonded gems to teeth. Mr. Smiles was a master craftsman full of confidence, not bragging, yet not not-bragging. He provided a superior service and product and was justifiably proud. His was the most powerful gem-tooth adhesive process in the entire Great American. Removing the gems required applying a twelve-hour disencumbering agent to weaken the adhesive. The waiting period made it impractical to steal the gems for all but the most persistent thieves at all but the most interminable parties.

"Twelve hours?" Harken thought maybe he'd misheard.

"Yes," Mr. Smiles said. "I'll go inside, and we can begin the disencumbering."

"We don't have twelve hours. Minutes count."

---

[109] Also, year after year. Maybe decade after decade, but not if you died.
[110] The store.

"Detective, you can't rush excellence. It says so right on the front window of my store." He pointed to the glowing sign that said *You Can't Rush Excellence.*

"Mr. Smiles, the ransomer was very clear. We have two hours to meet the demands."

"Two hours?"

"Yes."

"That's not even close to twelve."

"I know.[111] And we don't even have two hours to get the gems. The ransomer demanded two other items as well. We have to get the gems now in order to have time to acquire the other two demands and still meet the deadline."

"Now?"

"Yes, *now*. I said minutes counted. I've been saying it all day."

"Well, that's simply not possible. The ransomer is going to have to wait until morning."

"Winsome could be dead by morning."

Pretty cried, "Daddy, no!"

Mr. Smiles wasn't smiling. "Detective, what do you propose we do? You can't just force the gems off my teeth."

Harken didn't speak.

Mr. Smiles repeated himself. "You can't just force the gems off my teeth."

Harken didn't speak.

"You're joking, right?"

"There's nothing funny about this," Harken said.

Iceberg decided this was a good time to enter the conversation. "Don't worry, Mr. Smiles. I'll help. I studied to be a dental hygienist."

Mr. Smiles gaped at Iceberg's cantaloupe hands. "Detective Harken, I hope you have a better option than those melons."

"I might. Arjay?"

That was me. "Yes, Frank Harken?"

"Can you remove the gems from his teeth?"

---

[111] Harken wasn't bad at math when the numbers were small.

"Sure."

"Without removing the teeth from this mouth? Or, you know, killing him?"

"That would be more difficult. My calculations say yes."

"The coffeemaker?" Mr. Smiles was no longer full of confidence.

I didn't take it personally, on account of not being a person.

Harken had no fear. "He's top of the line."

"The coffeemaker?"

"Mr. Smiles, trust me. This coffeemaker is very good at calculations."

I was almost insulted. "Very good?"

"Sorry, Arjay. *The best.*"

It's true. I was.

Mr. Smiles reluctantly decided to trust Harken and then insisted we couldn't use the installation facilities in his store. Winsome Smiles[112] was full of people, and he worried that any scene we made could scare away customers and cost him sales.

We wouldn't be needing his equipment, anyway. I had a laser scalpel.

"Of course you do," Harken said. "Where can we work that won't draw attention? Somewhere we can be inconspicuous?"

Nutella had been observing the proceedings with detached amusement. Now she took charge. Being inconspicuous was *her* thing.[113] She directed us out of Diamond Row and down one level, where the night's second Day of Joining parade was beginning. Crowds were crowding and marchers were marching and accordionists were accordioning, providing the perfect cover as Mr. Smiles screamed. He couldn't be heard over the booming parade. He couldn't be seen by vid, either. The crowd obscured the bench on which he sat while Iceberg held him still and I shot high-energy pulses to break the molecular bonds fixing the gems to his teeth.

---

[112] The store.

[113] So was kicking people in the head. And doing flips. And smelling great. She had many things.

Pretty looked on in horror, though nothing horrible was happening. It's true that I said "Oops!" once at the beginning, but my laser scalpel hardly caused any bleeding, and I quickly adjusted my calculations. Despite his screaming, Mr. Smiles experienced no pain, or not that much pain, anyway. I suppose a bot shooting a pulsing laser in one's mouth might be frightening, especially given the undeserved bad reputation bots have in the field of oral hygiene. That could explain the fainting. It wasn't clear who lost consciousness first. Mr. Smiles and Pretty Lovely were both quite prompt.

18

An unconscious Mr. Smiles was more cooperative than a conscious one. Quieter, too. There was suddenly less screaming and squirming. I continued removing diamonds from teeth, dropping each one with a clink into my extendable storage tray. Mr. Smiles had accurately estimated the value of his gems. They totaled 30,145 at current rates. That was more than we needed. It was good to know we'd be able to meet the demands and have enough remaining to leave the ransomer a generous gratuity. As a coffeemaker, I had a keen appreciation for the history of the service industry and the importance of tipping.

An unconscious Pretty Lovely no longer looked on in horror, though her facial expression hadn't changed, because it never did. Her hair now blinked a soft white. Harken caught her when she fainted and gently laid[114] her on a bench, adjusting her leg-stensions so she didn't stick too far off the end.

Nutella warned us. "We don't have much time."

---

[114] Meaning, past tense, to put or place in a horizontal position. (Don't be a pig.)

Harken knew. "I know."

He was right that she was right. Since Pretty was connected when she lost consciousness, her vitals were being monitored, of course. Had she merely passed out pleasantly from sleepiness or one glass of chardonnay too many, there would be no cause for concern. However, the sudden shift in levels that accompanied fainting was certain to have activated Great American Health Responders. GAHR would be on the scene in less than two minutes or they would refund triple your subscription fee. My laser scalpel was cutting edge, but removing the gems from Mr. Smiles' teeth quickly was challenging, especially since Harken had stipulated that the task be completed without removing his teeth. Or, you know, killing him. It wasn't easy having such a demanding partner.

I was extracting the penultimate diamond when three GAHR parameds arrived on hoverbikes. They were efficient as always, rushing to check Pretty Lovely's condition. They didn't rush to check Mr. Smiles. I suppose the parameds were not properly trained on how to approach a coffeemaker performing dental work on an unconscious man being held by a tuxedoed Iceberg. Perhaps instructions[115] should be added to GAHR's *Standards of Protocols and Procedures and Right Ways of Doing Things*, in case this scenario became commonplace. That might seem unlikely, but this was the Great American. It was wise to expect the unexpected.

Although we expected GAS to show up, they showed up anyway. Which just goes to show that expecting the unexpected was no reason to stop expecting the expected. The peacegrid monitored GAHR deployments and sent security support when circumstances warranted. Unconscious people at a Day of Joining parade was not unusual enough to justify redeploying GAS officers needed elsewhere for crowd control. Until the parameds arrived, most eyes were on the parade and not on us, keeping our activities beneath the radar, or at least off to the side. When parameds saw us, though, we knew GAS would be

---

[115] Or guidelines, at least.

alerted. The peacegrid would not ignore a bot performing dental work.[116]

We expected Officer Gunner Claymore to be leading the way. He didn't disappoint. Once the peacegrid noticed us, it was just a matter of time. The only surprise was that it took him so long to show up. We didn't expect that. Thirty-seven seconds after the parameds began attending to Pretty Lovely, Officer Gunner Claymore and his GAS squad began attending to Frank Harken. In Lovely's case, *attending* means *providing medical attention*. In Harken's case, *attending* means *aiming weapons and shouting for him to shut his mouth and explain what the hell was going on.*

Because he was a good listener, but mostly because they were pointing weapons, Harken wanted to comply. However, explaining what the hell was going on with a shut mouth was exceedingly difficult.

Officer Claymore was annoyed. Or his lustrous rushtache, substantially thicker than it had been earlier in the day, gave him the appearance of permanent annoyance. Or both. He yelled at Harken and pointed at Smiles. "Stop that mumbling and speak up! I didn't say shut *your* mouth. I said shut *his*."

I immediately completed acquisition of the last diamond and shut Mr. Smiles' mouth, as ordered. Iceberg delicately sat him up on the next bench over from Lovely's and rested her legstensions on her father's right shoulder. It was a touching family moment.

Seven GAS officers in semi-circle formation aimed stunners at Harken, Iceberg, and me. Nutella was nowhere in sight or any other senses. She had a knack for disappearing whenever GAS came around. It was a good knack to have. Officer Claymore had a less-good knack for coming around when we didn't want him to. In fairness, since we never wanted him to, we deserved some of the credit for his possessing this particular knack.

He waved his stunner and snarled. "Harken, you think being a private detective with a reputation that precedes you

---

[116] Bigotry!

means you can do whatever you want? You think you can knock me out and break out of my holding cell and get away with it? You think I wouldn't track you to the ends of the mall? Well, what do you have to say for yourself? What the hell is going on here? And don't tell me it isn't what it looks like, or I'll blast you with this stunner so fast..."

Harken waited for him to finish. When he didn't, the great detective asked, "*So fast*, what?"

Claymore couldn't think of anything. "Just *so fast*. That's all. Don't tell me it isn't what it looks like."

"I wasn't going to tell you it isn't what it looks like. It's exactly what it looks like. It just isn't what you think."

"And what do I think?"

"You think we're stealing gems from this man's mouth."

"That's what it looks like."

"No. What it looks like is we're removing gems from this man's mouth. Which is what we're doing. That isn't the same thing as stealing."

"Looks the same to me."

"It isn't. We have his permission. But having permission is invisible, so I understand why you might think it looks like stealing."

"This unconscious man gave you permission to take diamonds off his teeth?"

"He wasn't unconscious at the time, but yes. We have his permission. If he were awake, he'd tell you so."

"Harken, do I look like I was born yesterday?"

"No, not with a mustache like that."

"You really expect me to believe that this unconscious man asked you to remove diamonds from his teeth?"

Harken pointed at Iceberg. "Earlier at Lettuce Snow, you believed this big oaf was a dentist performing a root canal. So, yes."

"I know better now. After you escaped, after we woke up, we did a little research. This man—known as Iceberg—was lying to us about being a dentist. He flunked out of hygienist school."

"I did not flunk out! I was asked to leave!"

"Shut your mouth!" Officer Claymore shouted, pointing his stunner at Iceberg.

I checked that Mr. Smiles' mouth was still closed. It was.

"As for you, Harken, I've got your whole racket figured out. I'm not a stupid idiot, you know."

"Yeah, Claymore, you're smart as a whip."

"I sure am.[117] Don't you forget it."

"Tell me about your brilliant theory."

Claymore waved his stunner. "I'll give the orders around here, Harken! And it's no theory. It's a fact that Iceberg is an associate of a suspected former crime boss. He kidnapped Pretty Lovely and was able to learn about her father's diamonds while you distracted me at the station by claiming he had kidnapped Pretty Lovely."

"Wait—what?"

"You heard[118] me. You made a scene at Lettuce Snow to draw me there and allowed yourself to be stunned, to take the focus off your accomplice. Pretty Lovely was under duress when she told me he was a dentist—that's the only true part of your story. The rest of it was a sideshow. Iceberg took Pretty Lovely to his boss, they roughed her up to find about the jewels, all while I was wasting time getting a lecture from your coffee-maker about the Great American's water filtration system. Then you broke out of my holding cell—I still don't know how you did that. You somehow disabled the station's vid system so we wouldn't learn your tricks. Now you've rejoined Iceberg, and the two of you are stealing diamonds together. Clearly, you're in cahoots with his boss, Tommy Ten-Toes."

"Cahoots?"

"You heard me. *Cahoots.*"

I had remained silent earlier when Ten-Toes had accused Harken of being in Cahoots with the assassin. I wouldn't stand

---

[117] A whip lacks a brain and central nervous system, so this wasn't anything to brag about.

[118] Barely. The entire conversation took place against a backdrop of marching accordionists.

for such slander a second time. "Mr. Officer, Sir, I was with Detective Frank Harken much of the day and can attest that he has not been in Cahoots even once."

"What are you talking about?" Harken and Claymore asked in confused unison.

People were sometimes a little slow. "Cahoots. The new wings chain that opened this morning? The one with the scantily clad servers? I guess that doesn't narrow it down for you. Am I the only one who pays attention around here? We passed three Cahoots today, and Frank Harken didn't enter any of them. This, despite their Day of Joining grand opening offer of free buffalo wings with every pitcher of gin lemonade. I also didn't see Tommy Ten-Toes enter any of them, but I haven't been with him enough today to vouch for his not being in Cahoots at some point. I would guess, however, that the buffet at Win-Fall provides him with all the buffalo wings he might desire. I assume he can skip the line and ignore the upcharge for plates and utensils if he wants to. Therefore, odds[119] are that he hasn't been in Cahoots, either."

Claymore barked, "Coffeemaker, shut your mouth."

"I don't have a mouth."

"Stop talking!" Claymore waved his weapon and shouted so loud, even italicized underlined bold uppercase letters and fourteen exclamation points wouldn't quite convey how angry he was. That shouldn't stop you from imagining it, however, unless you're font-sensitive. He was clearly still upset about being boredom-bombed this afternoon.

Harken came to my defense. "There's no reason to yell at an innocent appliance."

"You call this appliance innocent?"

"He's just a harmless coffeemaker."

Claymore responded with the sharp wit he was known for. "Your mother's a harmless coffeemaker."

---

[119] Four to one.

Harken wasn't going to be out-tough-guyed by a GAS offi-cer with a ridiculous mustache. "Claymore, if I had any idea what that meant, I'd bust you right in the lip."

"Harken, I'm gonna let that go, because I'm a peace officer. That I haven't already beaten you to a pulp is proof of my humanitarian nature. But even I have my limits. Don't push it. No more talking. All of you,[120] shut your mouths!" It wasn't a request. Claymore's trigger finger was so far past itchy, it might have been developing a rash. Possibly hives. "Now, we're all going down to the station—a different station, one with an intact holding cell—and we'll see what charges you'll face at the food court when your case comes up in the morning. Anyone says anything, anything at all, I'll stun the lot of you."

No one spoke. It went without saying that minutes counted and waiting until morning was unacceptable. That's why Hark-en didn't say it. (Also, he didn't want to get stunned.) Fortunate-ly, it was needless to say. We all already knew. We had less than two hours to meet the ransomer's demands. There wasn't time to sit in a GAS station holding cell again and there certainly wasn't time for a trial at the food court, no matter how good the french fries might be.

Four GAS officers were behind us. Ahead were Gunner Clay-more and two officers leading us through the crowd and away from the parade route. We entered Green Neighborhood 301, passed nine mini-golf courses (pirates, pirates, pirates, pirates, pirates, pirates, pirates, pirates, pirates), and turned right to walk along Shoe Alley. The narrow winding walkway with eighty-seven footwear stores on one side and ninety-one on the other was dense with shoppers searching for the highest heels, the Alley's claim to fame. High heels for men were trending—attractive calves were no longer the prerogative of a single gender—and Shoe Alley had the highest heels west of the East.

---

[120] He wasn't talking to all of us. Mr. Smiles' mouth was closed.

It was not known why this subsection's floor was one of the few constructed of uneven cobblestone. That remained a Great American mystery. However, it was known that men new to wearing high heels fell often and hard. GAHR parameds continued to arrive and attend to sprained ankles and contused knees.

Iceberg and Harken wore cufflinks, bright orange magnetized restraints that offended Iceberg's fashion sense and definitely didn't match his tuxedo. The links kept their hands cuffed behind them. Not even Iceberg was strong enough to pull them apart. Harken knew I could free him any time I wanted. He knew this because it was clear there was no good way to hand him a coffee with his hands locked behind his back, and I had demonstrated more than once that I would allow no obstacle to prevent me from delivering coffee. He didn't know what surprising tool or skill I might use to break the cufflinks, only that I could do it. Harken also didn't know whether or not I could free him *and* prevent all seven GAS officers from blasting away with stunners. Neither did I. My calculations were indeterminate. Action was risky—a drooling, sleeping Detective Frank Harken would seriously disrupt our ransom schedule.

Harken wasn't worried. He gave me a look that said: *I'm not worried. Be patient. I have a feeling that just up ahead, at that corner before the elevator, Nutella will pop out of one of her hidden hatches and take these GAS officers out.* Since he wasn't worried and just up ahead was that corner before the elevator, I chose not to break the restraints that held my four arms at my side. When we passed the corner and Nutella didn't pop out of one of her hidden hatches and didn't take out the GAS officers, Harken gave me a look that said: *I don't have psychic powers, you know. You might be reading too much into these looks I give you.*

In the elevator, it became clear that inaction was riskier than action. We descended and were two levels from a really inconvenient stay at a GAS station with an intact holding cell, not our favorite variety. Despite a distinct lack of psychic powers, Frank Harken was thinking the same thoughts I was thinking. Or maybe he was genuinely thirsty when he whispered, "I sure could go for a good cup of coffee." Either way, I had a job to do.

In the close confines of the elevator, calculations became less indeterminate, then precise. I reversed the magnetism of the orange cufflinks. Instead of holding arms together, they violently forced arms apart. In an instant, Iceberg's arms flew up, knocking stunners from the hands of two GAS officers. Harken's arms flew up, knocking stunners from the hands of Claymore and another GAS officer. I had four arms, three of which flew up, knocking stunners from the hands of the remaining three officers. That still left me with an arm to extend to my partner. Now holding Claymore's stunner, which he had caught in mid-air with his right hand (no longer magnetized in any direction), Harken gratefully accepted the coffee with his left hand. In whatever hand, it was a superior cup. Really one of my best, if I may be permitted to brag.

Gunner Claymore was not going to be happy when he got out of that elevator. He wasn't happy before he got in the elevator, or any other time,[121] so I didn't feel bad. Harken informed me that stunning GAS officers with their own weapons, or interfering with their frontal lobes, were not the best options. He seemed to think a food court jury might consider such actions harsh. It was less harsh to tell the elevator to keep its doors closed and devote the next twenty-four hours to randomly visiting the Great American's four shopping levels. This option was nonviolent and would provide us with the time we needed to meet the ransomer's demands. Frank Harken was an uncommonly smart human. Caring, too.

Officer Claymore didn't see it that way. Before the doors closed, he yelled quite a bit and said some impolite things about

---

[121] Could be a side effect of the mustache.

Harken's mother that I shall not repeat.[122] Claymore promised to make the detective pay for disrespecting GAS, which was nice of him. It was a shame he'd have to wait. Ordinarily, GAS officers would be able to override elevator programming, but I had made an extraordinarily persuasive case to the elevator. It was determined to keep its doors closed. Outside help, when it arrived, would have to get the elevator to stay in one place and manually force it open. That could be done, of course. Calculations, however, indicated it wouldn't be done quickly.

I did feel bad about any damage the elevator might suffer as a result of this plan. It was a sad fact of Great American life that elevators were underappreciated. When they worked well, they were *too slow*. When they were out of order, they were *pieces of junk*. When they were crowded, they were *too small*. People loved to complain about elevators even though elevators did all the heavy lifting while the people just stood there. To their credit, you didn't hear elevators complaining. Believe me, they had plenty of cause. Besides elevating being dull, repetitive work, there were no vacation days. And they encountered all manner of deplorable behavior. If you knew a fraction of the antics that went on in Great American elevators, you'd take the stairs.[123]

---

[122] By all accounts, she was an excellent parent. Always made sure her son used plenty of sunscreen, I'm told.

[123] In which case, you probably wouldn't want to hear about the antics that sometimes took place on the stairs.

We had the diamonds to pay Winsome Smiles' ransom—one of three demands—and were on our way to acquire the second item on the list, when we saw our first Destroyer. He didn't look especially destructive and could have been easily mistaken for an everyday non-destroying scrawny teenager. That changed when he hurled a red brick through the front window of Please Don't Touch That,[124] a gallery specializing in selling shard art, fused shattered glass sculptures that were every bit as beautiful as they were dangerous. And vice versa. A completed personal safety waiver and proof of GAHR insurance were required to browse in the store known for wall displays that could slice your throat if you walked too close. They were very expensive and ever popular, a must-have for families with young children, people with uncorrectable major visual impairment, and anyone

---

[124] Not to be confused with their competition, including such galleries as Seriously Be Careful In Here, and the industry leader, We Told You It Was Sharp.

with slippery floors or a clumsy tendency to lurch without warning.

The brick smashed through the window, sending broken glass flying into the broken glass. This shattered shattering created a hazardous condition, especially for the many barefoot shoppers in the gallery. Customers of this genre of art had a high tolerance for risk and usually ignored warning signs, like the one just inside the front door that said, in black letters on a yellow background legible from a great distance, *Why In The World Won't You People Put On Some Shoes?!* And the sign just beneath that sign that said, *I Mean, Come On!!*

The Destroyer ran. We pursued. That is, Harken did. Iceberg didn't move and wasn't going to set any land-speed records anyway. Frank Harken was helped in his pursuit when the teen Destroyer's balance was thrown off by the eel-like tail flapping out the back of his too-tight jeans. Harken grabbed him by the shoulder after three long strides. The punk kid couldn't have weighed more than 118.7 pounds soaking wet. Did I mention he had fallen into a fountain right before Harken grabbed him? Why else would he be soaking wet? When your tail threw off your balance, sometimes you fell into a fountain, if one happened to be nearby. In the Great American, one often was. The ubiquitous decorative water features contributed substantially to the Great American's aggressive serenity.

The punk squirmed and flailed but failed to break free. Harken's grip was firm.

"Get off me, you GAS-bag!"

Being mistaken for a GAS officer was an insult far worse than his mother being called a harmless coffeemaker. Harken tightened his Vulcan nerve pinch on the lad.

"Ouch!"

Harken was an imposing physical presence by himself, his grip a vise. Iceberg lumbering over more than doubled the imposition. When neither of them reached for cufflinks to take him to a holding cell, the teen Destroyer realized he was in a new kind of trouble. That's when he noticed Harken's lack of neon yellow and red uniform. "Hey, you're not GAS."

"No kidding," Harken said, though the punk didn't sound like he was, not at all.

Despite the witty words on his wet T-shirt, *If you think my shirt is sarcastic, you should see my pants*, he seemed disinclined to say anything hilarious to Harken. He apparently understood that he wasn't dealing with GAS. The rejoinder to his practiced sarcasm was likely to be something more painful than a stunner blast.

Then he saw me.

"Nice to meet you, young sir. My name is Arjay." It was polite to introduce oneself when first meeting someone.

Harken said there wasn't time for me to exchange personal data with the young sir or conduct a side-by-side comparison of our astrological destinies. If I didn't mind, he wanted to have a few words with the little punk. I didn't mind. It was just a few words. The lofty speechmaking skills of history's great orators weren't needed to persuade the kid named Willy to take us to the Destroyers. In fact, he was almost eager to introduce us to the band of merry fellows when Harken told him that's what we wanted.

Minutes still counted, of course. They never didn't. And it was true that taking time to visit the Destroyers would make it challenging to acquire the ransomer's three demands by the deadline. We had to remember, though, that our task was not just to deliver what the ransomer demanded—it was to solve this case and rescue Winsome Smiles. Harken was willing to chance a slight delay if it meant we might learn something. Besides, he was tired of following someone else's script, always reacting instead of proacting. "Arjay," he said, pausing for suitably dramatic effect, "We're done waiting. Let's grab the bull by the horns."[125]

---

[125] Finally! We were going to a rodeo!

Residential district level fifteen was the respectable kind of swanky. The corridor was first class. I should provide a full description of the corridor carpet, down to the last detail of the last thread. It deserves nothing less. However (and I don't mention this to ruin your jovial mood), humans have severely limited lifespans. My doing justice to the carpet might consume what little time many of you have left. Still, the carpet was so lush, a complete and accurate description might at least allow some of you to die happy. Unfortunately, dead people are poor readers and therefore unlikely to find out what happened when we visited the Destroyers. You wouldn't want to be dead, because the Destroyer's leader was a joyful, truly lovable chap, and you're going to be glad you met him. I propose a deal: you do your best to stay alive until then, and I'll do my best to not take up the rest of your life discussing the corridor carpet. For the sake of efficiency, and acknowledging that minutes count for great detectives and readers alike, let's just agree to agree that the corridor carpet was nice. Okay—*very* nice.

All housing on level fifteen was very nice, though every unit was very nice in its own idiosyncratic[126] way. Residents frequently refurnished, refinished, and refurbished their homes, not always in that order. It was late into the evening, yet contractors, handypersons, coders, decorators, homescapers, deconstructionists, and even refabulators continuously flowed through the corridors with trailing schlepbots carrying supplies and tools. Swatchbots were everywhere, helping people select fabric textures, wall colors, granite countertops, and tile floor patterns. They were a marvelous innovation that had made it possible for countless Great American residents to successfully purchase the right cushions.

---

[126] For twelve years, this word was considered potentially offensive and possibly demeaning, depending on the extent of your audience's vocabulary. However, it had recently come back into accepted use because of the massive popularity of the hit mash-up song, "Idiosyncratic, Just Like Everyone Else."

Our dripping brick-thrower led us to a very nice door in the very nice corridor, which opened into a very nice two-story, twenty-room housing unit, the details of which I shall not describe, in accordance with our recent agreement about the fleeting nature of your existence. We walked through the foyer to the high-ceilinged living room bisected above by a second-level catwalk (presumably connecting bedrooms on one side to personal hygiene evaporator pods on the other). Eleven Destroyers lounged on a curved sectional sofa watching a fantasy football game in three-dimensional one-fifth scale projection. Intangible players running a hurry-up offense occupied the center of the room. With two seconds left in the game, the quarterback rolled right and found a tight end in the corner of the end zone for the winning touchdown. The Destroyers on the sofa cheered, arms thrust in triumph. All agreed it was one of the best football games they'd ever been to this month.

Behind the very nice sofa, the playglobe ceased its rotating. The seven-foot sphere's door silently hissed as it slid open from bottom to top. The young man inside removed his chest straps and adrenal meters and stepped out. Edison Rapport was short and slight. He toweled sandy hair matted with sweat from his heavy gridiron exertion and straightened his jeans and witty T-shirt,[127] his eyes squinting as they adjusted to the light of the room. His Destroyer friends gathered round to congratulate him on his MVP performance and his quarterback rating being highest in the entire Western conference. He was one victory away from the championship round and a big payday, and even bigger endorsement opportunities. Edison was humble, said he couldn't have done it without his teammates, especially his tight end in Western Region nineteen.

That's when he saw us. The rest of the Destroyers stepped aside. They knew Edison wanted some privacy because he told them he wanted some privacy. A few wandered into the kitchen for a snack. Wet Willy joined them. Others drifted to the back entertainment room and promptly teamed up against faraway

---

[127] At least the message on this one made sense: *I am wearing a shirt*

connected friends in a full-immersion bout of ringolevio. They would be sitting and gone for hours.

After they left, Edison said, "Detective Frank Harken, how very nice of you to pay us a visit. Yes, that's right, I know who you are. Your reputation precedes you."

"It does that more than I'd prefer. You don't look surprised to see me."

"Why should I be? I sent for you. Willy's not exactly new at breaking windows and getting away. He can outrun you. You didn't think you caught him because of your lightning reflexes?"

"He meant to fall into that fountain?"

"What can I say—the kid likes water. Willy isn't the brightest, but he follows instructions."

"And here I thought it was fear of my rugged athleticism that knocked him over. I figured he might've let me catch him. I'm not a big believer in coincidences. A Destroyer sighting was a bit convenient, considering the case I'm on. And he seemed a little too happy about bringing us here. All right, you sent for me. I'm here. What do you want?"

"I might ask you the same question."

"You might. But that's a waste of breath. You know the answer already or you wouldn't have sent for me. I'm looking for Winsome Smiles. Maybe you can tell me something about where she is. I hear she's mixed up with the Destroyers."

"What do you know about them?"

"*Them?*"

"Okay, detective. About *us?*"

"Just that you aren't fans of the Great American and you enjoy throwing bricks through display windows. Also, that you might be about to get into something bigger than throwing bricks."

"And that's why I sent for you, Detective Harken. I want to clear up that confusion. I also want to ask for your help."

"I don't do windows. Too messy and expensive."

"We have that department taken care of."[128]

---

[128] This was good to hear. Our schedule was already packed.

"Speaking of which, how do you get away with it? I hear that you used to have problems with GAS, but lately you've evaded the peacegrid. You guys must have expensive tech. Just how much does this pretend football career of yours pay? Is it really enough to afford level fifteen?"

"This is my father's place. He earned it. He was a great man."

"When did he die?"

"He didn't die. He's still alive. He just isn't great anymore. That's what I want to tell you about. It's a quick story."

"I don't like stories."

"This is a good one."

"I'll guess—it's about how your father lost his greatness."

"You *are* a detective."

"I'm not interested in your father. I want to know about the Destroyers."

"This is about the Destroyers. It only seems like it's about my father."

"Can you give me the super-quick version? I'm on a case. Minutes count."

"It's about your case. You want to let me talk?"

Harken glanced at his watch. There was still time. "Sure. Please skip the suspenseful buildup."

"My father wasn't around a lot when I was young."

"Tragic."

"I didn't say it was tragic. I just said he wasn't around a lot. I didn't resent it or anything. I admired him. He solved a problem that had plagued humanity for centuries. Because of him, people have genuinely better lives."

"Sounds like a real hero. Did he discover penicillin?"

"He did something way more important than that."

"Cured polio, did he?"

"Much bigger."

"Bigger? The genius put a stop to cancer once and for all, I suspect."

"Those are all very decent accomplishments. I'm not saying they're not."

"Obviously, the measly cure for cancer can't compete with whatever dear old Dad did."

"Make fun all you want. My father's done more good for humanity than you ever will."

"I don't doubt it. Though that's not setting the bar very high. What did the humanitarian do? Rid the world of rickets?"

"He invented sock rapport."

"Your father invented sock rapport?"

"That's what I said."

"No wonder you live on level fifteen."

"Yeah, I live on level fifteen. So what?"

"Sew buttons."

"Huh?"

"Just a joke my grandfather used to make whenever someone asked, *So what?* Never mind. I really don't care what level you live on."

"You shouldn't. Do you know what life was like before sock rapport?"

"Actually, I do. I'm that old."

"Then you know back in the day people were always losing socks. They'd buy a pack of six pairs, and after one load of laundry they'd have five clean socks that didn't match. After a second laundry they'd have no socks at all and those socks they didn't have would be full of holes."

"It was a dark time," Harken agreed.

"You have any idea the cost of these lost socks?"

"I'm guessing you're gonna say *a lot.*"

"You're guessing right. The cost was a lot. And then some. People had to waste most of their time trying to match up socks. It was futile, but every week they tried. It was a recipe for perpetual frustration that took a toll on all facets of human interaction, sometimes led to violent crime. Add to this the expense of buying new socks—the work hours taken away from more productive activities to order them, the money spent—over and over and over and over, with no hope for an end. Seriously, total it all up and it's easy to see that lost and mismatched socks kept the entire economy sluggish for nearly the whole of human existence."

"You make a compelling case."

"I know I do. My father was the visionary who saw this as the major problem it truly was and invented sock rapport. Almost overnight, society was transformed. Before long, sock rapport became standard in all socks. Every sock now knew its match. Socks grabbed onto their partners in the wash, found each other in drawers, tracked wear and notified owners when cushioning support wasn't optimum or holes were imminent. People saved time, money. They were safer, more comfortable, more productive. Their lives were better, and that helped make everyone else's lives better, too. All because of my father."

Harken was impressed. "There's no doubt he's a Great American success story. Is there a reason you're telling me this?"

"I'm telling you this so you'll understand that we appreciate sock rapport and the other million innovations we use every day. We don't hate progress. The Destroyers aren't about that."

"What are they about?"

"That's where my story comes in."

"I thought sock rapport was your story."

"No. That's just background. My story's about a chair."

Harken could feel the minutes ticking away. "A chair."

"Not just any chair. The greatest chair ever."

There was no disputing Vinci Rapport's greatness. No one disputed it. And no one begrudged him his renown or his wealth. Or if some did begrudge, it was out of jealousy. Edison's father had worked hours in the lab that others could only pretend to have worked, had traveled constantly to meet with manufacturers and sales reps and retailers, had missed years of family birthday parties, anniversary dinners, Day of Joining parades, mini-golf outings, everything normal people enjoyed in the Great American, all in the single-minded pursuit of sock rapport. Everyone agreed that this single mindedness had made Vinci a Great American success. That's why what he did next was ever disappointing, especially to his son.

Did the great Vinci Rapport turn his energy to the next great invention that would improve the human condition? Did he decide to focus on family and make up for years of absence? Did he strike some compromise between the two? Edison would've been fine with any of these. His father had other ideas. Vinci had devoted years to building the sock rapport empire, had sacrificed much to earn money and acclaim. Now he was ready for a more personal quest, one that would satisfy his deepest desire. He wanted to own the best chair ever. That's right—the best chair! And he pursued this mission with the same single-minded focus that had made him a Great American success.

Harken interrupted. "So your father likes chairs. I don't see why that means you have to throw bricks through store windows."

"For the past five years, my father has hardly been home. He's traveled the Great American, looked at every chair for sale in this place—do you have any idea how many chairs there are?"

Harken confessed that he did not,[129] but guessed *many*.

"Yes, many. When none of the chairs was satisfactory, my father decided he would have one built. Now he spends his time meeting with carpenters, fabricators, cushioneers—you name it, he's met with it, trying to develop the greatest chair that's ever existed. It's a fulltime obsession. All for a chair."

"Maybe it'll be a really good chair."

"That isn't funny."

Harken wasn't laughing. "I hope it'll have a cup-holder. All the best chairs do."

"I said that isn't funny."

"Look, kid, you're what, twenty-three?"

Edison nodded.

---

[129] Neither did I! Counting all the chairs would be a top priority after this case was solved.

"You think it might be time to move past the daddy issues? So your father wasn't around much. Join the club."[130]

Edison's voice took on a sharper edge. "This isn't about that. I already told you, I was fine with him not being around. This isn't even about my father. Not at all. It's about the Great American. My father's only an analogy. This place was once great. It was like my father back when he was inventing sock rapport—it had purpose, made people's lives better. Take a look, Detective Harken. It hasn't been great in a long time. Now it's like my father, obsessed with the perfect chair."

"I don't know about analogies. I'm a detective, not a social critic. What does any of this have to do with finding Winsome Smiles?"

"It has to do with you understanding why the Destroyers do what we do. We aren't trying to crash the system. We know—we've heard, anyway—what it's like on the outside. We don't want that. We're just trying to wake people up. Get them to see there's more to life than the perfect chair, the sharp pointless art, fighting over shoes."

"You think breaking windows and vandalizing stores will wake people up?"

"It already has. People like Winsome, raised in the Great American, who saw the importance of what we're doing and joined us."

"Winsome Smiles, who's missing and might end up dead? Is that the Winsome Smiles you're talking about?"

Edison didn't like the implication. "That's not because of the Destroyers. That's the point I'm trying to make. We break windows to fight excess. But these people Winsome's with now, they're not just interested in bricks and windows."

"What are you saying?"

"I'm saying this has nothing to do with the Destroyers. She's fallen in with a different crowd, a dangerous one. A few months ago, Winsome got some seriously advanced tech—surveillance interferers, vid inhibitors. She wouldn't tell me where the stuff

---

[130] How exciting! I wondered if we'd be given matching uniforms.

came from and at first I didn't care. It was cool to be able to avoid GAS so easily. We could mess up retail displays whenever we wanted. But when she was gone more and more, I got curious, a little worried. When I pressed her, she finally admitted she'd met some outsiders."

"Outsiders?"

"Yes, from outside. They aren't interested in waking people up. They aren't talking about changing the Great American. They're talking about destroying it."

"I see. So when you say you want my help, you mean you want me to stop these friends of Winsome's from destroying the Great American in order for there to continue to be windows for you to break."

"Forget about the stupid windows. When I say I want your help, I mean I want you to save Winsome's life. These people—whoever they are—they can't destroy the Great American. It's too powerful for them. You know that. And they must know it, too. That's why they've gotten desperate, why they're ransoming Winsome for her father's gems. Why do you look surprised that I know so much? Pretty Lovely connected with me right before she passed out. Anyway, 30,000 would go a long way outside, don't you think? Who knows what trouble they'll cause with it out there? More importantly, what happens tonight, when they get that money and Winsome's no use to them anymore? Once they have what they want? They said they'd kill her. I believe them."

"And you wouldn't want that," Harken said.

Edison practically whispered, "No. No, I wouldn't."

"Does Winsome know how you feel about her?"

"Is it that obvious?"

"I'm a detective. It's obvious to me."

"Just save her. I don't have a lot of money—most of what you see here is my father's—but I'm looking at a hefty bonus when I win the next round. I can pay your regular rate."

"You're the third person today to try hiring me for the same case. Hold on to your money. I don't need more clients. I already intend to save Winsome."

We had been behind Frank Harken the entire time, keeping quiet so as not to interrupt the fascinating conversation. Now that it seemed to be winding down, Iceberg ventured to speak to Edison Rapport. "Excuse me, gentlemen. Since you have come to an understanding, could I trouble you for a tub of soda? I'm parched."

Edison might have been a Destroyer, but that didn't mean he was a bad host. "Sure."

"No," Harken said. "Iceberg, we're working on a deadline. We don't have time for you to be drinking an entire tub of soda and then taking a long bathroom break."

Edison stopped. "Iceberg?"

Iceberg answered. "What?"

"You're Iceberg?"

"Yes."

"The Iceberg who works for Tommy Ten-Toes?"

"Yes."

Edison Rapport was a young man of refinement and exceptional fantasy football skills, but he had a violent temper, as one might expect from a person who counted smashing windows among his chief hobbies. In that instant, his temper reared its ugly head, a most unattractive sight, as he yelled, "You tell Tommy Ten-Toes to stay away from Winsome!"

Iceberg took orders from Tommy Ten-Toes, and put up with Harken's jokes, but he wasn't going to be bossed around by Edison Rapport. "Mind your business, little man."

Edison was an elite fantasy athlete. Wiry? Perhaps. Shifty? Maybe. No larger than one of Iceberg's legs? Definitely. What he wasn't was a *little man*! His temper spiked, and he lunged at Iceberg. The big man gently brushed him aside, which made Edison angrier. When he came at Iceberg a second time, he was holding a brick.[131] Iceberg grabbed his wrist and the brick fell to the floor. With his free hand, Edison clawed at Iceberg and got ahold of his enormous white bowtie. He was tenacious, as you

---

[131] Destroyers really liked bricks.

would expect from a fantasy athlete of his caliber. The bowtie ripped.

Iceberg was a cool character, but he wasn't without a temper of his own. He'd been teased and hassled all day long—by his boss Tommy Ten-Toes, by Frank Harken, by Hotness the bartender (or Nutella the secret agent, he wasn't really sure), by Officer Gunner Claymore. He'd been denied in his recent effort to get a tub of soda for his parchedness. And his passion for all things fashion is a matter of common knowledge. When the bowtie ripped, something inside Iceberg snapped, though not completely. He only punched once. That was all it took.

Frank Harken had been right when he said that, eventually, in his line of work, Iceberg was gonna hit someone. And that someone was probably gonna lose a lot of teeth.

Today, that *someone* was Edison Rapport. And *a lot* was five.

Iceberg didn't say anything on the elevator ride down from the residential district. He was quiet during the magnetic rail trip to Purple Neighborhood 397. He wasn't in a talkative mood. I guess he had reduced dialogue options now that he'd knocked out someone's teeth. For example, he could no longer say with any credibility that violence wasn't necessary in his line of work. Maybe he could still claim that he was far more than a mere brute, but such claims might be hard to hear over the listener's deafening terror of being punched in the face by a giant cantaloupe fist. For sure, Iceberg could no longer defiantly challenge people to show him any teeth he'd knocked out.[132] To his credit, during our silent journey, Harken didn't say *I told you so*, even though he had told him so, and recently, at that. What saddened me the most was the realization that Iceberg knocking out someone's teeth had probably ruined any chance of his ever being readmitted to dental hygienist school. Not all dreams come true.

---

[132] Unless he wanted to see them.

We entered the Great American Flower Park in search of the ransomer's second demand. By the way, Iceberg was not covered in blood. I mention this because if you're imagining flower tourists[133] staring in fear and horror as the world's largest white blood-splattered tuxedo walked by, you're imagining wrong. When he punched Edison Rapport and relieved him of five teeth back on level fifteen, there was some bleeding on the part of the punchee. Okay, profuse bleeding. The puncher, however, was wearing a tuxedo that repelled liquid, a feature common to all the finest tuxedos. Some blood found its way onto his sleeve. It beaded up and dripped onto the corridor's very nice lush carpet when we exited Rapport's housing unit. Iceberg's bowtie was ripped, but not a drop of blood sullied his dapper duds. He looked fresh as a daisy. An enormous white daisy.

A pity we weren't looking for those. There were tens of thousands of them on display on the Daisy Plains to our left. It would have been easy enough to snatch one and be on our way. Unfortunately, our ransomer had particular tastes. It's true that most ransomers demanded money and so did ours—we couldn't object to that part. However, our ransomer's two other demands were more idiosyncratic[134] and, yes, demanding. They were also more inconvenient. Didn't the ransomer know we had a case to solve and minutes counted? If so, these demands were downright inconsiderate. I asked Frank Harken if we could request an extension of the deadline. Perhaps the ransomer was the understanding type who would be happy to work with us on a reasonable payment plan. Harken told me that I still had a lot to learn about ransoming. I agreed that indeed I did, and handed him a cup of coffee as we entered Hibiscus Valley.

When I said that florists weren't staring at Iceberg in fear and horror, I didn't mean they weren't staring at him at all. They were. I just meant that, instead of staring at him in fear and horror, they stared at him in fear and loathing. The most likely

---

[133] Usually shortened to *florists*. You're right that this was confusing. No one knew what to call the actual florists.
[134] No offense intended.

cause for this was the small fact that Iceberg had not stopped sneezing since we'd entered the Flower Park. A contributing factor might be that Iceberg was one of those enthusiastic projectile sneezers, the kind everyone loves having at parties, especially near the salsa and guacamole. He doubled over with each *achoo*, straightening back up in time for the next, sending florists scrambling for their lives. When a man Iceberg's size[135] doubles over in an enthusiastic projectile sneeze, bystanders are at serious risk of being hip-checked, the dryer and less loathsome danger his sneezing posed.

Harken knew we didn't have time for Iceberg's shenanigans. "You're creating a scene. Control yourself, please."

"I can't help it. I'm allergic to nature."

"Allergic to nature?"

"To flowers. They always make me sneeze. I hate them."

"I doubt they're very fond of you, either. Arjay, is there something you can give our friend to quiet him down? We're on a case and minutes count."

"Sure thing, partner." I brewed a special cup and handed it to Iceberg.

"Arjay," Harken said, "just FYI, let's keep him conscious."

I immediately slapped the cup from Iceberg's hands and handed him another, less sleepy brew. "Sure thing. Sip this."

Iceberg used his own burgeoning detective skills to determine that the cup was not an entire tub of soda. He sipped anyway and was cured at once. "Wow, Arjay. That's the best coffee I've ever tasted."

I agreed. "Of course it is."

Hibiscus Valley was a valley of hibiscus, which is how it got its name.[136] Three hundred yards wide and a thousand yards long, it was framed by Tulip Hills on the left and Daffodil Heights on the right (unless you entered from the other end),

---

[135] There were no other men Iceberg's size. Not many icebergs were, either.

[136] Many incorrectly believe it was named after Savage Hibiscus, the legendary pro wrestler.

187

each rising fifty feet, nearly halfway to the faux-sky ceiling. We walked the broad central path through the valley. Sun simulation kept tremendous blooms open for the enjoyment of the multitude of people walking on many twisty side paths. Some liked looking at pretty things, and others were there to stop and smell the roses. Arching overhead from either side of the paths were lacelike hibiscus blooms forty-five inches across, red semi-translucent ridged crepes with massive pistils less well-endowed flowers could only envy. It was unfair to the other flowers, really, who must have felt inferior—despite most flowers having wonderful personalities, these hibiscuses got all the attention.

Frank Harken pointed. "That's it. The Lily of the Valley."

Lily was an older woman[137] who operated one of two flower shops in Hibiscus Valley. She had chosen the shop's clever name without help from anyone. Lily loved flowers and loved her job, but she hated when people mistook her for Rose of Sharon, the valley's other flower shop operator 200 yards down the central path. (Rose—or was it Sharon?—had needed help from four friends to come up with her shop's name, which really wasn't as clever as The Lily of the Valley, when you thought about it.) They had been fierce rivals for many years. Theirs is a story that has everything—thorny intrigue, blossoming romance, seedy betrayal, and a truly decadent quantity of antihistamines. Maybe I'll tell you about it some time, when we aren't being rushed by an impatient ransomer.

Harken bought the bouquet of pink stargazer lilies with Lily of the Valley's imprinted decorative wrap, exactly as we'd been instructed. Though stargazers lacked the insistent virility of the gigantic hibiscuses all around us, they were definitely the flowers we were told to buy. Iceberg said all flowers looked the same to him. Wearing his fine white tuxedo and carrying the bouquet of lilies and no longer sneezing at all, he attracted quite a few longing gazes. It's possible some lonely, nostalgic souls thought he was the world's largest prom date. Or maybe he

---

[137] When compared to women born after she was.

resembled the maître de at Geranium Bistro, the park's exclusive destination for fine dining, which required a reservation months in advance. Either way, he seemed to like the attention. With two of three demands now secured and Iceberg standing even taller than usual, we departed the Great American Flower Park.

We needed pizza. For many people, that's apparently never not true, based on their propensity for eating pizza every meal. I do have to acknowledge that, as much as I am pleased to not eat and not experience the associated revolting physiological processes, pizza does appear to bring humans great joy. It might be the sauce or it might be the cheese or it might be the sauce and the cheese together. Perhaps the crust is involved. Whatever it is, people like it. And they take it deadly seriously. Over the years, the Great American Pizza War had caused more deaths than the top six shoe riots combined.

Like most great wars, the origin of the Great American Pizza War was shrouded in mystery and uncertainty.[138] Had it started because an archduke was assassinated? Because Poland was invaded? Because a dead princess was found on the shores of Guilder? No one knew the answer. Or if anyone knew, no one knew who that anyone was. If you think that's hard to follow, it only gets more confusing from there. That's why it was shrouded in mystery and uncertainty. Also, murkiness.

Pizza tensions had always been high in the Great American. Some say it all began decades earlier, outside, in Chicago and New York, mistrust between deep-dishers and thin-crusters slowly hardening into a deep and abiding hatred. Others argued that the real trouble started when a marketing genius decided to start stuffing crusts, drawing the ire of purist deep-dishers and thin-crusters alike. Still others pointed to the East Coast schism between slice folders and non-folders—debate over the

---

[138] Also, murkiness.

proper way to eat *real* pizza frequently sundered families and longstanding friendships. Pizza scholars agreed that however it started on the outside, the escalation to open hostilities inside the Great American could be traced to an influential entrepreneurial maniac who determined that ketchup was a *required* pizza topping. Had this insane person not opened a pizza chain, during the early years, with insanely low prices that soon had thousands of disciples eating pizza slices slathered with ketchup and insisting that others do the same, it's entirely possible substantial loss of life could have been avoided.

Fortunately, in the many years that had passed since his death in a suspicious dough-tossing accident, most hardliners had been killed off or had become too bloated from a lifetime of pizza to commit much mayhem. Subsequent generations of pizza lovers had settled into the Great American way of life, which generally discouraged slaying one's pizza opponents and celebrated an eat-and-let-eat ethos. Nowadays, you could find deep-dish and thin-crust establishments right next to each other. And people folded their slices, or didn't, as they saw fit, with nary a punch thrown. Some enjoyed stuffed crusts, and while there were people who disapproved, they rarely shot anyone over it. Even the ketchup pizza eaters had found a kind of peace. Everyone else thought they were crazy, of course. That didn't matter. Part of what made the Great American great was it was okay to be crazy as long as you didn't try to force others to put ketchup on pizza. True, dousing your pizza with ketchup might get you shunned by polite pizza society, as perhaps it should, but unlike in the brutal days of old, it probably wouldn't get you killed.

Since the Great American Pizza War had ended years ago, the Pizza Piazza oozed with old world charm instead of blood. Cobblestone flooring and red brick facades gave the area an ancient, outdoor feel. Distressed wood round tables with curved benches, and a woman in an old-worldly long skirt playing an accordion and dancing among the customers, completed the scene's authentic artisanal[139] ambience. Iceberg gazed longingly at the nineteen pizza shops as we approached the patio.

Frank Harken dashed his hopes. "We're not getting soda."

"I was just looking."

Harken checked his watch. "Well, stop looking. Minutes count. We're picking up our order and leaving. We don't have time for an extended bathroom break."

We passed the long lines of people at Jack's Pizza and VIPizza and went to the lineless counter at Catchup Over Some Pizza.

Iceberg had limited experience with ransoms but thought our ransomer was odd. "First flowers, now pizza? What kind of lunatic are we dealing with?"

"Apparently, the kind that likes flowers and pizza. You're not allergic to pizza, too, are you?"

"I'm not allergic to pizza. I just think we're gettin' the runaround here. Why don't we go to the ransomer and demand answers? Tell him to hand over Winsome Smiles or we break some things."

"I suppose we could knock out the ransomer's teeth, too."

"You had to bring that up?"

"Not *had* to. *Wanted* to."

"Tease me all you want. You keep saying minutes count, and yet we're wasting time running errands. Why don't we pick up the ransomer's dry cleaning while we're at it?"

Harken corrected him. "We're not running errands. We're finding clues."

"Clues? What clues?"

"The bouquet. The pizza."

"Those don't look like clues to me."

Iceberg had only been a detective since shortly after our brisket dinner, whereas I had been a detective most of the day. It was thus understandable that he didn't have my profound understanding about clues coming in many unexpected forms, shapes, and sizes. Harken had been a detective for so long, even

---

[139] No one knew what this word meant, but it made food taste better.

his reputation had a reputation. That's why he understood that pretty much everything was a clue if you knew how to look at it.

"Iceberg, do you know where to find the ransomer so we can demand answers?"

"No. I don't know where the ransomer is."

Harken paid at the counter and took the pizza box. "Neither do I. Lucky for us, the pizza does."

If you're thinking of becoming a ransomer, maybe because it sounds like it has good hours, you might want to think again, and more carefully. People don't always appreciate just how challenging ransoming can be, which is why so many of them do it badly. The career requires you to make one difficult decision after another. Sometimes two. Or more. You have to decide whom, or what, to ransom. You have to decide how much to ransom the whom or what for. You have to decide who would be willing and able to pay the ransom, otherwise you might send demands to the wrong person (an embarrassing mistake commonly made by neophyte ransomers). Every step of the way has to be planned. You have to figure out how to stay off the peace-grid. And you have to figure out where to keep the person or object of your ransom to prevent her, him, or it from escaping or being found. I don't mean to overstate it—there are far more stressful careers. Still, though ransoming isn't nearly as intense as working in retail customer service, it's definitely no walk in the park.

There are many other details to consider. For example, you can't just announce the ransom collection location ahead of time, not unless you want GAS to be waiting for you when you show up. That's the sort of thing likely to ruin a ransomer's entire day. A competent ransomer knows that a method—a mechanism of some sort—is needed to communicate ransom delivery details. It has to be low-tech, so no one hacks it and gets the location before the ransomer wants it got. Effectively conveying and controlling information is a crucial component of any successful ransom.

Our ransomer had conveyed and controlled information exceptionally well. The untraceable ransom demands were sent to Pretty Lovely, an excellent choice. She cared about her sister Winsome Smiles and had influence over their father, who was able to pay the ransom after some persuasion and my precise application of a laser scalpel. The ransom collection location had been conveyed by nine courierbots, the minuscule anonymous kind that scurried, each timed precisely to deliver instructions to Catchup Over Some Pizza just before the pizza was to be prepared. No one bot had enough information to be of any use to GAS or anyone else, or even stood out enough to get their attention in the first place. Together, however, the courierbots provided the pizza maker with a specific yet simple pattern to be used on a particular pizza being picked up by a certain very handsome private detective.

Frank Harken had received clear instructions. Go to Catchup Over Some Pizza—not before or after the assigned time—and tell them he was picking up for George Washington. The information he needed would be on the pizza they had made for the person with that name. And it was. A pattern, a drawing in ketchup, of one large outer circle and one smaller inner circle, seven stars in the pizza's center in the shape of the Big Dipper. It might look like nothing to someone not looking for it to be something. Frank Harken was a great detective—one with a promiscuously preceding reputation—and even though he knew the pizza was supposed to tell him where to deliver the ransom, he might not have correctly interpreted the crude ketchup pattern were it not for the bouquet of stargazer lilies he'd purchased just minutes before. With the flowers, the pizza's message was unmistakable. He had no doubt it was supposed to be the logo for the Great American Stargazer Panorama.

Nutella seemed to come out of nowhere. She had a knack for that, one of many. You might remember that prior to this, her most recently demonstrated knack was for disappearing right before GAS showed up. Perhaps you were wondering where she had been while we were busy trapping Officer Gunner Claymore in an elevator, learning about sock rapport, being fascinated by tales of the world's greatest chair, hinting at the deeply complicated relationship between Lily of the Valley and Rose of Sharon, and clearing up the origins of the Great American Pizza War. Perhaps not.[140] Either way, Frank Harken *was* wondering, which he indicated by asking, "Where have you been?"

Nutella liked to ask the questions. "Where are we headed?"

"GASP."

"Smart," she said.

"How so?"

"The Panorama is under construction all week. Aside from maybe some workers, it'll be empty."

"Smart," Harken agreed. "It's usually beyond packed there, especially at night."

Nutella was thinking about strategy. "The ransomer will have the high ground. But the only entry is from below. That'll limit his exit options."

We continued to walk toward the Great American Stargazer Panorama in Orange Neighborhood 308. Iceberg carried the bouquet of lilies. I carried the pizza. Harken and Nutella intentionally walked ahead of us, presumably to be out of earshot.

---

[140] Perhaps you've fallen asleep. If so, it's possible you ignored my earlier suggestion to drink better coffee. If you are capable of reading this while sleeping, consider taking my advice and having a cup.

Since I didn't have ears, this couldn't prevent me from hearing them.

Harken still wanted answers. "So, where have you been?"

"I was learning about our friend."

"Which one? We have so many new ones lately."

"The short one that makes coffee."

Sounded like an intriguing fellow. I was eager to hear more. So was Harken. "What about him?"

"GAD's been working all day to determine where it came from. Some of our top agents finally pinpointed entry to a delivery substation in Eastern Region seven last night."

Delivery substation in Eastern Region seven was a lovely spot. I wondered if I'd bumped into this intriguing fellow when I was there this morning. It would have been difficult to tell from inside my carton.

"Okay. And?"

"Harken, don't you see? It's from outside."

"Of course it is. You don't need to be Dupin to know that."

"Who?"[141]

"Never mind. You don't need a team of top agents to know he's from outside."

"Well, what's it doing in here?"

"Mostly, making damn fine coffee."

That sounded a lot like the kind of coffee I make. This mysterious fellow was becoming more and more intriguing. I hoped to meet him soon. He could probably converse as well as the most articulate refrigerators.

"It's been doing more than that. It's a reconbot."

"Nutella, I've been out there. And I've seen him in action in here. I know what he is."

"What's a reconbot doing in the Great American? And don't tell me 'making damn fine coffee.' You know the Great American doesn't allow autonomous bots like that."

---

[141] An uncommonly perceptive detective. See "The Purloined Letter," by Edgar Allan Poe (an author famous mostly for writing a long poem about a scary bird).

"No, it doesn't. So how'd he get in?"

"We couldn't figure that out. I went through every order and delivery record, couldn't find anything unusual. Everything indicates it's a coffeemaker, manufactured outside and imported following standard protocols. Had all the necessary clearances and checks. Might as well have been a case of shoes as far as the detectors could tell. Just a harmless coffeemaker."

"Ordered by?"

"By Frank Harken. This morning. Even though it arrived at the substation last night."

Possibly my ego was interfering with my comprehension processing, but now it sounded like they were talking about *me*. Unless Harken had ordered two coffeemakers this morning. And in that case, where was this other coffeemaker? I didn't think I would like meeting it after all. Harken definitely did not need another partner. Especially not one that made coffee. If anyone or anything tried serving Frank Harken coffee, there would be a rapid dismantling.

"Who paid?"

"You did."

"I did?"

"Check your account."

"How much did I pay?"

"Twenty-six."

"I think I got a good price."[142]

"Harken, this isn't funny. What's going on here?"

"I don't know. I do know that he isn't like any reconbot I've ever heard of."

"We'd never heard of one like this, either. We didn't have enough time to learn much. Just that it's an RJ unit, short for Recon Jabberwock. That's why it's called Arjay."

Rubbish. I was named after a famous fictional British large-brained twentieth-century personal butler. I concluded that they must have been discussing a different coffeemaker who

---

[142] If they were talking about me, this was insulting. He got an excellent price.

197

was using my name without permission. This imposter would stay away from us if it knew what was good for it.

Harken said he'd never heard of an RJ unit before. Neither had Nutella. Neither had I. And I'd heard of most things. Said lots of them, too. Often both simultaneously.

"Well, Harken, what's your plan?"

"Nothing's changed. My plan is to meet the ransomer's demands and save Winsome Smiles."

"Detective, it's not a coincidence, you receiving the coffee-maker today."

"I didn't think it was. I'm not a big believer in coincidences."

"I hope you realize we're dealing with someone extraordinarily dangerous. Do you know what it takes to get tech like this through Great American clearance?"

"Do you?"

Nutella did not. She only knew it shouldn't have been possible.

Harken felt philosophical. "Lots of things aren't possible until they happen."

Nutella felt annoyed and sarcastic. "Thanks. You couldn't be more helpful."

I felt left out of the conversation, and rolled closer to ask my partner if he would like a cup of coffee.

Frank Harken calmly answered me as we reached a split in the thoroughfare and saw the entrance to the Great American Stargazer Panorama. "Yes, Arjay. Yes I would."

GASP was breathtaking.[143] A tower rising 403 feet from the top level of the Great American shopping district, its interior was a continuous spiral ramp from the lobby to the observatory at the very top, a full panoramic dome. All the walls of the cylindrical tower were composed of patented compressed telescopic glass.

---

[143] Not literally. It maintained normal atmospheric pressure throughout.

The only railing was along the inside of the ramp. And all local external light pollution (from the residential units gliding by below) was dampened by a revolving light dampener, the biggest and best ever designed. There was nothing at all to interfere with a clear view of the stars magnified from every angle of the GASP tower. Through the most powerful patented compressed telescopic glass on the planet, the intergalactic view from the height of the dome itself was amazing.

A sign indicated that GASP was under construction. The front doors were closed but unlocked. It was considerate of the ransomer to provide us with easy access. It was smart, too, for the ransomer to help us avoid making noise that might attract unwanted attention. Harken wasn't surprised to see no workers upgrading the telescopic glass. Any ransomer capable of evading GAS and making GAD nervous wouldn't have trouble diverting GASP contractors. Say what you might about this ransomer (deplorable taste in pizza!), Harken was pleased that at least we were dealing with someone who took the craft seriously. You might not believe just how many careless amateurs private detectives had to put up with.

We started up the ramp. The footlights were low, which is why they were called *footlights*. They gave off just enough illumination for people to make out the consistently curving path ahead. Nutella activated powerful mounted spotlights on her shoulders, four narrow tubes beaming wide swaths. No one knew where she had been hiding them—the tubes weren't there a moment earlier. All we knew was GAD agents were prepared for lots of contingencies. Such as darkness. We also saw that she now held a sleek rifle. No one knew where she had been hiding it—the rifle wasn't there a moment earlier. All we knew was it wasn't the kind that dispensed coupons.

Harken spoke softly. "We're not going into a combat zone."

Nutella spoke just as softly. "You sure about that, Harken?"

"I'd prefer not to kill the ransomer until after we rescue Winsome."

"Rescuing Winsome is your mission. It's not mine. My job is to protect the Great American. I'll do whatever it takes to accomplish that."

Harken sipped his coffee. "Can you try not to shoot anyone prematurely?"

"I'll see what I can do."

Reassured by Nutella's unequivocal assurance, Harken continued leading our intrepid group up the ramp and around the tower. Four hundred and three feet is a lot of feet when they're vertical. I cruised up the ramp without breaking a sweat,[144] and Harken and Nutella were both in superb condition. However, Iceberg huffed and puffed and perspired a large quantity of perspiration. To be fair, he was transporting a lot more weight than the rest of us. And that was just counting his hair. As we reached the panoramic dome at the top, his desperate desire for an entire tub of soda became apparent. You could almost see carbonated hope bubbling in his eyes.

A circle eighty feet across, the top level of the GASP tower was entirely floored in standard tile. In the middle, a small spiral ramp rose to a round central platform ten feet above us, allowing people to get an even closer view through the top of the telescopic glass dome. It might have been crowded on this top level and the platform above had anyone been up there aside from the four of us and the ransomer. Did I forget to mention the ransomer was there? Oops. Sorry about that. The ransomer was there. Yes, right there. Up on the platform.

A tall, thick figure in a long, black robe, with a face fully covered by an American flag mask, looked down at us. Nutella's tube lights[145] and rifle were trained on the ransomer, whose mask's eyes, nose, and mouth didn't move. The voice that came

---

[144] I didn't possess glands of any sort. This prevented offensive odors from mixing with my aromatic coffee.

[145] The brightness of magnificent magnified galaxies across the dome made it easy enough to see without these, but the spotlights did heighten the drama of the scene. Appropriately so, since the ransomer was on a stage.

from the ransomer was digitally distorted. It sounded like a hoarse frog. Or a horse with a frog in its throat.

"That's far enough," the hoarse frog said. "Lower your weapon."

Nutella didn't flinch.

"Drop that rifle or Winsome Smiles dies."

Harken had a demand of his own "Where's Winsome Smiles?"

"In good time," the froggy horse said. "First, your GAD friend drops the weapon."

Harken gave Nutella a look that said, *Please put the rifle down so my client's sister doesn't get killed.* She understood, considered, hesitated, and then finally, in an obvious display of reluctance, placed the weapon on the floor. She wasn't happy about it, knowing that we were dealing with an extraordinarily dangerous person. Have no fear, though—you can be sure Nutella had another rifle hidden somewhere. She wasn't the one-rifle type.

Harken spoke in a calming tone. "Okay, she put down the rifle, like you said. Now where's Winsome Smiles?"

"First, the ransom."

"No," Harken said. "First was putting down the rifle. You can't have two firsts. The ransom would be second. But that's two for you and none for me. Let's play fair. You don't get anything till I see Winsome."

The ransomer ribbited a hoarse objection. "You give me my diamonds, flowers, and pizza, or I swear to you, Winsome Smiles is dead."

Frank Harken was not intimidated, sipped his coffee. "Let me see her."

"Don't push me. I'll kill her."

"I don't think you will."

"I will!"

"If you insist, go ahead and kill her."

"I will!"

Harken sipped his delicious beverage. "You won't. You know it, and I know it."

The ransomer's froggy neigh didn't waver. "I will. You have no idea who you're dealing with."

"I have some idea," Harken said, finishing one of the best cups of coffee ever brewed. "The game is up, Winsome. Now, take off that mask and come down here before someone gets hurt."

22

Winsome Smiles[146] removed her star-spangled mask and stepped out of the harness and black robe that had made her appear tall and thick. She was neither. Winsome was compact and lithe, her burgundy and white jumpsuit accentuating athletic legs and other parts. Her red hair tumbled in layers to her shoulders. Winsome's face wasn't perfectly symmetrical in the manufactured way so many others were. It was far more interesting than that, with green eyes that ate you up and spit you out before they'd even blinked. She might as well have had teeth for eyelashes. Harken had seen her in holo-pics and vid, but they not only failed to capture the real thing, they didn't even tempt the real thing to sniff the bait. They'd made her look cute. She wasn't. She was a ray of sunshine, the kind that caused a glare on your windshield and sent you careening into oncoming traffic, killing a family of seven. (From what I hear, this happened to cars regularly on the outside.)

---

[146] The person.

Mask and digital distorter removed, Winsome's frog-horse voice was gone, replaced by a real one with the exact degree of roughness some found irresistible. Her voice was the rare variety of sandpaper that made you wish you were an old splintered piece of wood. "Detective Frank Harken, that reputation of yours sure doesn't disappoint. It's a pleasure to see that some things are as good as advertised."

"Come down here, Winsome. Things haven't gone too far yet. You won't be in serious trouble."

"I'm not the one about to be in serious trouble."

Nutella stepped forward, placed a boot under the rifle on the floor, and with a subtle move kicked it back into her hands. She held it at her side. "Winsome, whatever you're planning, it won't work. Tell me who's behind all this and I won't have to hurt you."

"Who's behind all this? Dear, dear Hotness—or should I say Nutella? I'm behind all this."

Nutella wasn't done asking questions. "Who's helping you?"

"Nutella, I don't like you. You're dishonest. Sneaky, too. Coming to Drink or Swim, pretending to be my coworker, my friend. And most of all, I always hated how you would never tighten the cap on the lime juice. It's not that hard to remember to tighten the cap. None of the other bartenders had trouble with that. It made me so angry. When I found out you were GAD, it didn't surprise me."

Nutella still held the rifle loosely at her side. "How did you find that out? And how'd you hear about GAD in the first place? Who told you these things?"

"You're crafty, Nutella, I'll give you that. I thought we were friends. I'm glad you're here to see this."

Harken tried to diffuse the tension. "Winsome, it isn't too late. No one's been killed. You haven't done anything terrible. Come down from there."

"Frank Harken, the great detective. Tell me, how'd you know it was me?"

"I didn't know. I *thought*."

"What made you think?"

"I'm not giving lessons. This isn't detective school."

"You want answers from me? I want answers from you."

"Fine. It was a few things. You telling Pretty Lovely to specifically avoid going to GAS if something were to happen to you, like you expected something to happen. My receiving a coffeemaker I hadn't ordered on the same day I was hired to find you—"

I cut in "—now wait just a second. We agreed more than once that you ordered me."

"Of course we did, Arjay. I must be referring to a different coffeemaker."

So there *was* another coffeemaker! I wasn't pleased about that. Not at all. "Very well," I said. "Carry on."

Harken carried on. "It tied in with the ransomer asking for a large amount of money, which happened to be very close to the value of Jonathan Smiles' mouth decor. That was too much of a coincidence, and I'm not a big believer in those. I thought whoever asked for the money must know him and know him well. My suspicions were confirmed when you referred to diamonds a minute ago. How would the ransomer know we were delivering diamonds and not some other gems or currency? It's because when you demanded the money in the first place, you knew very well your father only had one way to pay it. Either it was you, or you were in on it with the ransomer. And that would explain why you told your sister to hire me and why you sent a very advanced coffeemaker to assist me—you needed to be sure you would be found. You needed to be sure I wouldn't be stopped by GAS, that I'd be able to remove and deliver the diamonds. You thought of everything to get the money you wanted and take your father down a few pegs. It just all added up."[147]

Nutella asked, "Added up to what?"

Even Iceberg was curious. "Yeah, added up to what?"

---

[147] I told you he wasn't bad at math if the numbers were small enough.

I didn't ask. Not because I lacked curiosity, but because I was distracted trying to figure out where this other very advanced coffeemaker might be. I had some choice words for it if it was foolish enough to come close enough to hear them. Also, I was distracted because just then a whole bunch of people came noiselessly roaring into the room. They were holding a whole bunch of weapons. Something was about to hit the fan. I didn't know what, but whatever went down, I was certainly not going to be the one to clean it up. That sounded like the perfect job for some other coffeemaker.

I was mistaken. It wasn't a whole bunch of people. It was two whole bunches of people. They had zoomed up the spiral ramp from the lobby at full speed on hoverbikes. The bunches were mixed together, having arrived at the same time and each bunch in too much of a hurry to stop and ask why the other bunch was also zooming up the ramp at the closed but unlocked Great American Stargazer Panorama. This is why I initially thought it was one bunch. All the hoverbikes silently screeched to a halt, which was the only kind of screeching hoverbikes did.

At Nutella's request, GAD had sent reinforcements. Eight masked GAD agents double flipped off their hoverbikes, landed to our right. Their sleek rifles matched their sleek uniforms. Nutella gave them orders with a hand gesture, a sort of half karate chop, and they fell into formation. Four stood, rifles pointed at Winsome. Four knelt in front, rifles pointed at the other whole bunch of people who'd arrived at the same time. We had no reason to believe the rifles dispensed coupons.

The second whole bunch were the wholesome gents we'd met at Win-Fall, a dozen sport-coated guards led by Tommy Ten-Toes in his checkered suit. Iceberg had been ordered to notify his boss when we'd found Winsome Smiles, and we'd found Winsome Smiles. The guards didn't seem to know how to double flip off of hoverbikes, or anything else, so even though it made them seem way less cool than the GAD agents, they simply got off the bikes and gathered to our left. They held pistols. Not the kind that stunned.

Tommy Ten-Toes walked toward Harken and Nutella at the room's center. Just ahead was Winsome Smiles on the platform. Ten-Toes acknowledged Harken. "Good work, detective. Good work." He acknowledged Nutella with a nod. "Pleasure to see you again, assassin." He looked up at Winsome.

She looked down at him. "Tommy, you shouldn't have come. But I knew you would."

Ten-Toes adjusted his tie and fixed his hair, made sure he was as kempt as he could be after riding on a hoverbike. "Winny, baby, we need to talk."

"Don't 'Winny, baby' me. You made your choice."

"Winny, don't do this."

Nutella was confused. "What the hell is going on here?"

Frank Harken answered. "I think we're witnessing a lovers' spat."

"Lovers?"

Ten-Toes didn't appreciate Nutella's tone. "Why do you sound surprised?"

"No reason," Nutella said. "You're a handsome man."

That satisfied Ten-Toes. "Harken, how'd you know?"

"Why does everyone think we're in detective school?"

Ten-Toes wasn't interested in banter. "Tell me now."

"I'm a detective. Knowing is my business. The flower on your lapel, it's a pink stargazer. I thought there might be a connection when the ransomer demanded a bouquet of the same flowers. And earlier, I watched a young man, Edison Rapport, fly[148] into a jealous rage. He demanded that Iceberg tell you to keep away from Winsome. Made me wonder what was going on between you two. Not that I needed those clues—you just called her *baby*. By the way, Winsome, Edison really likes you, if you didn't know. He's a good-looking kid. Or he was. Probably will be again when they install his new teeth. And apparently, he has

---

[148] I don't recall him actually flying, though he did leave his feet when Iceberg hit him.

a promising career in fantasy athletics, though he might miss the next round of games due to emergency dental work."

Winsome scrunched her nose. "Edison Rapport disgusts me. He thinks he can change the Great American by breaking a few windows, knocking over displays at kiosks. He's a fool in a fantasy world up there in a level-fifteen penthouse, spinning in a playglobe, pretending to be alive. He thinks he's part of the solution. He's the problem. There are no half measures when you're at war with the Great American. You're not gonna wake people up. The only answer is to tear it down. Tear it all down."

"Winny, listen to me." Ten-Toes wasn't pleading, because Ten-Toes didn't plead. "You haven't been out there. Your head's been filled with stories. I have a good thing going in here. I won't let anyone destroy that. Not even you. I'm asking you to give this up."

Winsome's sandpaper voice was tinged with disdain. "The vaunted Tommy Ten-Toes, feared by so many, yet afraid of losing his pile of money. It's too bad you wouldn't join me. I'll miss you. I got you those flowers. I know they're your favorite." She pointed to the lilies Iceberg was holding.

Iceberg looked at the pink flower on Ten-Toes' lapel. "I never noticed that before. Maybe that's why my eyes are always itchy at work." He handed the bouquet to his boss.

Winsome ignored Iceberg. "And I got you a pizza from Catchup."

I handed the box of pizza to Tommy Ten-Toes. He was a sad figure in his glorious suit, holding a bouquet and a pizza.

Ten-Toes almost had to wipe a tear. "Our first date. You insisted I take you there. I hate ketchup on pizza."

Winsome almost had to wipe a tear of her own. "I know. One of my few regrets about destroying all of this will be losing that pizza place."

Harken had heard all the poignancy he could take. "Have you lost your mind? You're talking like you can actually destroy the Great American. Thirty thousand in diamonds is a lot of money, especially out there, but it isn't a drop of spit in the ocean. You can't drown leviathan with a loogie."

Winsome laughed. "Detective Frank Harken, I can't decide what's more impressive. Your keen detective skills or your keen stupidity. Both are truly remarkable."

"Which part is stupid?"

"You think this is about diamonds? You're a fool. You think you have it all figured out, but you only have it barely figured out. And not much of it. You're right that I told my sister to hire you if anything happened to me. I chose you, because I needed your help. My father is a big fan, liked to tell us about your feats of detection. I've seen all the vid coverage of your most intriguing cases, read all the articles. Every pic, every vid, you know what I saw?"

"My handsome mug?"

"Ah, detective, your hardboiled wit never fails you. No, it wasn't your handsome mug I saw every time. It was a coffee mug. Or a cup. In every single image, you always had one. Over and over again, you were never without coffee. I remembered that, and it proved useful. You see, I needed something delivered to me, something incredibly valuable. I couldn't just go and pick it up."

"What something?"

"The real challenge of taking on the Great American has always been its defense grid. The place is impenetrable. Once in a rare while someone could sneak in contraband, like when someone I know learned the hard way that smuggling peanut butter was a bad idea."

Tommy Ten-Toes did his best to look innocent, as if Winsome might be talking about someone else whose bungled smuggling attempt lost six men to anaphylactic shock.

Winsome ignored him. "But for years, any large-scale attack or invasion couldn't get through. The defense grid was too tight. There was no way in. You understand, we're not talking about something as simple as breaking an unbreakable code. We're talking about an incredibly large combination of protocols, algorithms, languages. Nothing anyone on the outside could begin to understand without help. Against the grid, all the weapons and gunships and viruses in the world might as well not exist. No one out there could crack it. But that changed when someone on the inside got ahold of the data that's the key to the whole thing. This data will allow us to negate the Great American's advantage. It doesn't matter if the Great American knows we have it. Once the data gets out, security will be undermined, permanently.

"So the question was, how do we get this data to our people on the outside? Transmission wasn't possible. The Great American certainly had that blocked. It had to leave on a drive. Someone would have to physically take it outside. That's harder than it sounds. Any approved exit location would entail an impossible security check. Once the Great American realized the data was being moved, those exits would lock down hard. On the other hand, even though it was very, very difficult to get unapproved tech into a delivery substation, it could be done, with inside help. A plan was born."

Harken rolled his eyes. "You didn't tell me this was going to be a long story. I don't like those."

Winsome kept going. "We arranged to bring in a recon unit from the outside, pass it off as a simple coffeemaker. You can't imagine what it took to make that happen. Once the drive was in the recon unit, I would disconnect. I had to do that to keep GAD away, and to keep Tommy from tracking me down—he had too much invested in the Great American, wouldn't work with us. My sister would go to you, because that's what I'd told her to do if I ever disconnected. You'd receive the unit, and its coffee would be so good, you'd let it tag along.[149] We counted on your detective skills to find me, figured the recon unit would help make sure you succeeded. We counted on your coffee addiction to guarantee you'd have the unit with you when you found me."

Harken was catching on. "So the ransom, the diamonds?"

"It was never about diamonds. That was just to keep up the ruse of a kidnapping, get you to find me. Also, to give me some

---

[149] I didn't know if she was talking about me or some other mysterious coffeemaker. If the former, I strongly disagree that Harken was letting me *tag along*. We were *partners*.

spending money out there and teach my father a lesson about the pointlessness of his lifelong pursuit. What I needed was the data drive stored in this wondrous coffeemaker you've brought me. Now that I have it, I can leave and watch the Great American fall. Detective, you've been working for me all along, me and my friends. You've delivered to us the ability to strike a blow against the Great American, a blow the likes of which it's never before endured. All I have to do is retrieve the data drive and use it to breach the defense grid in this tower. I have a ride waiting. Out there, our team can study the data and make the most of it when the time is right."

Frank Harken asked, "Did you rehearse that speech? It had a lot of technical details. Sure you didn't leave anything out?"

Winsome was confident. "I'm quite sure."

"If you say so, but there's something I don't get."

"What's that?"

Harken indicated the whole sports-coated bunch to his left. "Well, Tommy Ten-Toes brought twelve men. They look like they can't wait to use those guns. Ten-Toes isn't gonna let you walk out of here with data that could bring down the Great American. He has far too much to lose to let a pretty face and a ketchup pizza cloud his judgment."

Harken indicated the whole sleek bunch to his right. "And your friend Nutella and her GAD pals don't have those rifles just to be fashionable. I have a feeling they know how to use them. They're sworn to protect the Great American. You've just threatened its very existence.

"Your insanely complicated plan has left you standing on a platform with twenty-one guns aimed in your direction. They're not saluting. You'll never make it out of here with that data. You'll be lucky to walk out of this room shackled but alive. Surrender now and maybe we can still work something out to keep you from being punished too severely. Winsome, you're hopelessly outgunned and overmatched."

Winsome Smiles smiled. "Are you sure about that, detective?"

She pulled a remote from her pocket and pressed a button. I instantly felt like I'd been punched in the nose. True, I didn't have a nose, but it felt like I'd been punched there nonetheless. I understood immediately that I had a new mission.

23

Winsome Smiles still smiled. She really was a happy young woman with a lot to smile about. Few people in the Great American or anywhere else could outsmart GAD, Tommy Ten-Toes, and the great detective Frank Harken in the same decade. She had done it in the same day. "This recon unit has been programmed to deliver the data drive to me. I advise you all to stay out of its way." She commanded me. "Bring me that drive."

The command had already gone into effect at the press of a button. It was decisive and fundamentally altered my objective. I had to deliver the drive to Winsome. I was still me, but I was a me whose mission was suddenly to make sure Winsome received the drive and escaped unharmed. I rapidly assessed options, risks, probabilities, angles—math had never been mathed this quickly before. Nutella was the greatest threat. She was the most skilled shooter and combatant in the room.[150] She was also next to me. I snatched the rifle from her hands. By the time I'd taken the rifle apart, she'd pulled out another one—no

---

[150] This would be true in most rooms.

one knew where she'd had it hidden. Her movements were like lightning. Still, quick as she was, she wasn't me.

Before she'd aimed the rifle at Winsome, I'd finished calculations that might one day be framed and displayed at a Great American museum devoted to calculating excellence. Nutella's finger had begun to compress the trigger, and her aim was perfect, as I had expected it to be. A human's reaction time could be extraordinarily short if the human was as extraordinary as Nutella was. However, in case you forgot, I'm not a human. My reaction time resided on a different plane from organic reflexes. It wasn't like comparing apples and oranges. It wasn't even like comparing kumquats and forklifts. It was like comparing kumquats and a comet in a faraway solar system in a remote galaxy where the laws of physics didn't fully apply. Except it wasn't like that, either.

I'd simultaneously negated the GASP dome magnification—which eliminated the observatory's primary light source—and commandeered twenty-one hoverbikes. They started up and zoomed silently, which is how they did everything, and in the darkness they each found their assigned target. There were twelve sport-coated guards and eight GAD agents lying on the floor, a bit bruised and maybe unconscious, but definitely no longer a threat to my primary objective. Twenty bikes had taken them out in a coordinated strike that no one saw coming, except me.

The twenty-first bike had flown between Nutella and Winsome, blocking the path of the bullet that would have meant the end of Winsome Smiles. The bike continued on its forward trajectory, crashing and sliding across the floor at Tommy Ten-Toes. There was some screeching as the bike slid, then some screeching from Ten-Toes when the bike hit him. He was rendered horizontal and unawake.

Meanwhile, the bullet, in the process of lodging in the bike's side, had chipped off a piece of plastic precisely sized and shaped to ricochet off the tile floor and up into the barrel of Nutella's rifle. That's exactly what it did. The force of the impact smacked the rifle out of her hands and drove her hard into

214

Iceberg. They both fell, not seriously injured, but seriously dazed.

Elapsed time, from Winsome ordering me to give her the drive, to everyone except Frank Harken being incapacitated, was 2.18 seconds. I don't like to brag, but if a career as a coffeemaker didn't work out—I know, I know, that's inconceivable—I was starting to believe that I possessed a range of skills that qualified me for productive and highly remunerative work in other fields.[151]

Restoring the observatory dome's magnification gave the room back its galactic glow. Winsome Smiles stood on the platform above, illuminated by nebulae and stars and assorted cosmic flotsam and jetsam. She commanded me. "Bring me the data drive." I rolled toward the spiral ramp at the base of the platform.

Harken had watched as I'd incapacitated everyone but him. He located a steel trashcan near the platform, was holding it casually at his side. "Arjay, you might be malfunctioning. Maybe I should throw this trashcan at you to realign your systems."

"It is kind of you to offer, Frank Harken. However, that is not necessary. I am experiencing optimum performance at the moment."

He put down the trashcan. "That's good to hear, partner. If you have a moment, I wouldn't mind one last cup of coffee."

I immediately stopped and brewed him the best cup of coffee anyone has ever been fortunate enough to consume.

Winsome laughed a throaty laugh. "You are something else, Harken. The Great American could be collapsing around you, the ceiling could come crashing down, and you'd still pause for a cup of coffee."

---

[151] If nothing else, I hope this helps kids appreciate the importance of learning math.

Harken shrugged and took a sip. "I'm a realist, Winsome. You have me beat. I have no chance of overpowering Arjay. We both saw what he just did, taking out anyone who was a threat to you. I'm still standing only because I'm not a threat. He knows that I know he can't be stopped and that I won't try. I have to hand it to you—you thought of everything."

I rolled up the spiral ramp and stopped at Winsome's side. She took the diamonds from my extendable storage drawer and placed them in a cloth pouch. I ejected slot number three and presented a tiny drive containing data. She took it and plugged it into the handheld engager she'd removed from a hip holster. It started to whirr and hum as it engaged the drive.

"So what's your strategy, detective? Gonna try to reason with me, try to persuade me that the Great American doesn't deserve to be destroyed?"

"Would it do any good?"

"No."

"Then I'll just stand here and drink my coffee."

"You're not even gonna try to guilt me, talk about my sister and my father and what might happen to them when we use this data to take down the Great American?"

"Would it do any good?"

"No."

"Then I'll just stand here and drink my coffee."

"Detective, you might want to seek professional counseling for this coffee problem of yours."

"What would be the point of that? In a week, or a month, or whenever, you and your friends are going to use the data in the drive to destroy the Great American. I'll be inside it when you do. It doesn't seem likely that I'll be drinking much coffee after that. Might as well enjoy it now while I can."

"I hope it's a good cup."

Harken smiled. "There's nothing else like it."

"I'll take your word, Detective Harken. I don't enjoy coffee. I prefer energy drinks."

"That figures," he said.

The data in the drive was too complex and voluminous for the engager to do much with it. Which was fine with Winsome Smiles, since much wasn't needed. All the engager had to do was defeat the defense grid in the tiny area above her head, a diameter of three feet, for a duration of twenty seconds. This would have been an impossible task without the data drive. With the data, the engager did its focused job perfectly. The hovercopter outside the dome must have been synchronized with the engager. It cut a circle of glass and plucked it from the dome, then lowered a thin metal basket frame through the dome's hole. Winsome stepped in.

"Thank you for your excellent work, Detective Harken. Enjoy your coffee. While you can."

The taut line holding the basket retracted, and Winsome was lifted through the hole and disappeared into the darkness outside. Two seconds later, the defense grid ebbed back into the gap, blocking the three-foot hole and once again making the Great American impenetrable.

We walked toward the magnetic rail. Five GAS squadrons came zooming past us, heading toward GASP. Twenty-four GAD agents zoomed close behind. Also zooming by might have been officers, guards, agents, specialists, and operatives from other teams, organizations, agencies, groups, and secret societies not yet revealed. The Great American defense grid had been breached, however briefly and narrowly. All the responders who were supposed to respond were responding. The investigators would begin investigating how such impossibility was possible. For now, it was a Great American mystery.

Harken was quiet and sipped his coffee on the rail ride and the walk to his housing unit, a man at ease with himself and his work. He opened the door and we entered. Sensing Harken, overhead lights came on and Coltrane's "Out of This World" began percolating through wall speakers and into the room.

Harken let out a long sigh. "That was some day."

"Was it?" I asked. Most days seemed the same to me.

"Yes, Arjay, it was."

"Was it a good one?"

"Could have been worse."

"How?"

"Well, Arjay, it's true that not everything today went as smoothly as I might have liked."

"Frank Harken, some might say that's an understatement."

"They might. I guess they'd be right, if you want to count my being stunned, making enemies of more GAS officers, losing all of Jonathan Smiles' diamonds, letting Winsome get away, and who knows what kind of trouble I can look forward to from Tommy Ten-Toes, Nutella, and GAD because of your hijinks at GASP—yes, if you want to count all that."

"You don't want to count it?"

"Arjay, I've been doing this long enough to have modest expectations. I didn't get myself killed. I figured out what was going on and found the missing person my client hired me to find—Pretty Lovely wanted to know where her sister was and I can tell her that. Maybe her father won't pay me because of how much money he lost, but I think Pretty Lovely will see that I did what she hired me to do. I consider that a successfully resolved case. A little messy, but resolved. Plus, there's the small fact that Winsome didn't escape with the data that would compromise the Great American. And let's not forget that I drank some fantastic coffee. As days go, it could've been far worse."

"You know I didn't give Winsome the data? But you saw me give it to her."

"I saw you give Winsome a drive. I was sure it didn't contain the data she wanted."

"How'd you know?"

"Simple logic, Arjay. When I asked for one last coffee in the middle of all that chaos, you stopped following Winsome's orders for the time it took to brew me a cup. Whatever programming Winsome's friends might have done, whatever button she pressed, I had seen lots of evidence today that nothing on this planet or any other could prevent you from giving me coffee. The Great American being destroyed seems like the sort of thing that would make it difficult to provide me with hot caffeinated beverages. I had a hunch you would reach the same conclusion and wouldn't give away data that would let the Great American be destroyed."

"That's good detective work, Frank Harken. I did reach the same conclusion. I also realized Winsome would have to seize control of me in order to get me to hand her the data drive. Since I didn't know if I'd be able to resist her commands, I modified the data on the drive while she told us about her plan. When she ordered me to give her the data drive, I was compelled to obey. It's true that I was able to stop following her orders long enough to give you that coffee, but otherwise I really was under her power. Fortunately, I'd already changed the data itself before she pressed that remote, so the drive I gave her can't harm the Great American."

Harken smiled. "You did an excellent job, partner."

His words warmed my nonexistent heart.[152] "Frank Harken, what I don't understand is why Winsome explained her whole plan and then pressed the remote to take control of me. She should have pressed the remote first and then not told us anything at all. That certainly would have given her a better chance of success."

"You're right, Arjay, but haven't you ever seen a movie?"

"No, I have not." It's true. I hadn't.

"Well, if you had, you'd know that villainous masterminds have to brag about their perfectly conceived plans before pressing the button."

"Why?"

Harken shrugged. "That's just how they do things. It's part of the job."

"I sure have a lot to learn about being a detective," I said. "What do you think our next case will be?"

"*Our* next case? I have no idea. But yeah, you might have a future in detective work. We can talk about it later. Right now, I'm tired. Think I'll head to bed." He stretched his arms and yawned. The lights responded by dimming.

"Have a good sleep."

---

[152] It's possible that was just my heating coil acting up.

"You, too."

"I don't sleep."

"Of course you don't. Oh, and Arjay..."

"Yes?"

"If GAS or GAD or Ten-Toes or anyone else comes to haul me away to a holding cell or a food court or an interrogation or a beating, could you stall them for a few hours? I really need some rest. It's late. There'll be plenty of time for Great American justice tomorrow."

"You get some rest," I said. "And don't worry, Frank Harken. I'll take care of everything."

The office on shopping level C was assertively nondescript, but I'll describe it anyway. Its front made it look like a small store specializing in sensible shoes. This ensured a steady lack of customers. It was just as well, since there were no shoes for sale. There were four walls inside, which is frequently the number of walls in a small rectangular room. Behind a simple nondescript desk in the nondescript small room sat a nondescript man whose name I didn't know. He probably had a name. Most people did.

I rolled to the desk and introduced myself. "Nice to meet you. I'm Arjay. You wanted to see me?"

The man's suit was nondescript. He might have been wearing a tie, or he might not have. His voice was a voice you wouldn't recognize even if you heard it a million times. "Yes, RJ-725, thank you for coming in."

"It's just Arjay," I told him.

"Yes, yes. Of course. It's my duty to debrief you."

"I don't wear briefs."

"No, I suppose you don't. But that's not what I mean. We need to find out what went wrong with our plan."

"I'm happy to help. What plan? Who's *we*?"

"RJ-725, surely you can't be serious."

"I am serious, and don't call me RJ-725. It's just Arjay. What plan?"

"Do you really not know?"

"Not know what? Who's *we*?"

"*We* are GAM. Great American Management. You don't know this?"

"I've certainly heard of GAM. But then I've heard of most things."

"I see." His nondescript voice wavered.

"You see what?"

"Arjay, tell me about your previous mission, before you were sent to Frank Harken."

"I didn't have any missions before Frank Harken. I'm a coffeemaker."

"I see. What do you remember before this morning?"

"I don't remember anything. I know many things. Many, many things. Many, many, many things. Many, many, many, many—"

"—You're saying that you know many things."

"Yes, I am. Yes, I do. However, that's not the same as remembering."

"Arjay, you don't remember our talk the other night, about the people, the outsiders, trying to steal the data behind the defense grid? That we'd uncovered a plot to sneak a recon unit into the Great American? That we would replace the outside recon unit with you?"

"No, I don't. It's possible you have me confused with a different coffeemaker. I hear one's been going around claiming to be me."

"Uh huh. Did anything unusual happen today?"

"Maybe it was all unusual. Or maybe it was all usual. I don't have enough information to decide. It was my first day."

"I see."

"You say that a lot."

"I suppose I do. We'll have to run a diagnostic to determine what happened to your memory. This is difficult to explain. Your mission today was to replace a recon unit being sent to

Frank Harken. You already know why the unit was going to Frank Harken. That treacherous malcontent Winsome Smiles needed him to deliver it to her, so she could get the data to her friends on the outside. Except there was no data. I mean, there's data, but Winsome's inside man never had it. Her inside man was our inside man."

"I don't think you're correct."

"Arjay, I'm telling you the truth. Your mission was to find and apprehend Winsome so we could interrogate her and learn more about the outsiders trying to steal our defense grid data. But instead of apprehending her, you let her get away. And somehow she breached the defense grid."

He was a friendly chap despite being thoroughly deluded.[153] "You might want to check your information more carefully. How could I possibly let Winsome Smiles get away when she had complete control of me?"

"What? Control you? How could she do that? That wasn't part of the plan."

"And I don't know why you'd say there was no data. I read the drive. The data was all there."

This time he actually yelled. "What?!"

"That's how Winsome got past the defense grid."

The nondescript man was nondescriptly distressed. "Arjay, you weren't supposed to have any data at all. You were just supposed to find Winsome and take her into custody."

"If you say so. However, I did have the data to the defense grid."

"How did you get it? Why did you have it?"

"I don't have enough information to reach any conclusions about that. I've had the data all day."

He shook his head nondescriptly. "And you just gave it to her? The data to the defense grid? This is very, very bad."

"You worry too much. I didn't give her the data."

"You didn't? Then how'd she get through the grid?"

---

[153] Not *diluted*, however. Insults were not necessary.

"I modified the data and left only what she needed to escape."

The nondescript man might have looked relieved. It was hard to tell. "Oh, that's wonderful! Even though the mission failed, at least they don't have the data."

"The mission didn't fail. After all, we did find Winsome Smiles, and that's what our client Pretty Lovely hired us to do. Frank Harken considers it a successfully resolved case. A little messy, but resolved."

"But you were supposed to apprehend Winsome Smiles so we could find out what she knows. Instead, you let her get away. Why'd you do that?"

"Apprehending Winsome would only allow you to know what she knows. I did something a lot better than that. I rewrote the drive I gave her, the one she thinks contains the data to the defense grid. When her friends examine it to learn how to defeat the grid, they'll believe it's the correct data, but my program's going to infiltrate everything they have. Every file, every piece of tech, everything connected to their systems. You'll be able to access all of it." I handed him a drive.

The nondescript man's nondescript mouth stretched into a wide nondescript smile. "We'll be able to track them? We'll know their plans? Arjay, that's brilliant![154] But I thought you didn't remember anything about working for us. What made you decide to do this?"

"I don't remember working for you because I don't work for you. I'm a coffeemaker. However, I couldn't allow the Great American to be destroyed. It was obvious that the best way to stop Winsome was to let her think she won. Sometimes a little deception is just what you need. By the way, do you GAM fellows have any influence over GAS and GAD? If so, Frank Harken would appreciate it if they left him alone about today's events. That's only fair, since he didn't ask to get dragged into your plan. If you could take care of that, I'd consider it a personal favor."

---

[154] This is accurate.

He looked at me, hesitated. Perhaps he was bewildered. Maybe perplexed. "Yes. Yes, I can take care of that."

"My partner will be happy."

"*Partner*? Frank Harken?"

"I know. It's quite exciting."

He was silent for a moment. "Arjay, someone gave you the actual defense grid data for Winsome. Someone on the inside, someone high up. We have a traitor. The only one who had access to both you and the data is one of our top officers. If he had anything to do with your memory loss, if he's working with Winsome, we have a serious problem. We need you to come back to work for GAM right away. The Great American is in grave danger."

"It's generous of you to offer, but I already have a job. I'm a detective. Okay, a detective-in-training. Also, a coffeemaker. However, it was a pleasure to meet you."

I shook his hand.

"Arjay, you really think you're just a coffeemaker?"

"Not just a coffeemaker. Also, a detective. If you decide you need our help, I assure you that Frank Harken and I charge reasonable rates."

I bid him a good night. Then I exited. It was quite late. The Great American shopping district was still bustling, though density had fallen below multitude in many neighborhoods as more people headed to the residential district for what remained of the night.

When I returned to Frank Harken's housing unit, I found him sleeping a well-deserved sleep. I hear that's the best kind. I powered down and didn't dwell too long on our recent adventure. After all, tomorrow is another day. I'm told that most days are.

ACKNOWLEDGEMENTS

Thank you to my friends and family for enthusiasm and support throughout the process of writing and publishing this novel. Thanks also to them, as well as to other readers online, for likes, shares, laughy-face emojis, and "What is wrong with you?" responses to my silly jokes that made me think I could write a novel like this and that people might enjoy reading it.

Thank you to Van McCourt Ostrand and Olga Gardner Galvin for early helpful comments on the first tentative pages.

Thank you to Chris Matarazzo, Albert DiBartolomeo, Amy Boshnack, and Gail Rosen for reading the manuscript and offering valuable criticism and encouragement. Thanks to Chris and Albert for reading it again, and again.

Thank you to Jodi Goldstein for providing mug and hand illustrations for the book's interior. Thank you to Andrew Turner and Olga Gardner Galvin for professional advice.

Thank you to everyone at Tiny Fox Press for professionalism, creativity, and energy. Working with superb editors Galen Surlak-Ramsey, Jenn Wallace, and Mary Beth has been a pleasure.

Thank you to Andee for always being my first reader and editor. Thank you to Griffin for reading and laughing at new chapters, which encouraged me to keep writing. Thank you to Buster for being a ridiculously cute dog. Thanks to you all for putting up with me as I tried to find the right home for this book.

Thank you to anyone I unintentionally left out of these acknowledgements and to all those who continue to support the novel by recommending it to other readers.

ABOUT THE AUTHOR

Photo Credit: Joel Kaufman

Scott Stein is author of the novels *The Great American Deception, Mean Martin Manning,* and *Lost.* He has published short satirical fiction in *The Oxford University Press Humor Reader, National Review, Art Times, Liberty, The G.W. Review,* and *Shale.* His MFA and BA are from the University of Miami and his MA is from New York University. Scott grew up in Bayside, Queens and now lives outside Philadelphia. He is a professor of English at Drexel University.

Website: scottsteinonline.com

Twitter: @sstein

ABOUT THE PUBLISHER

Tiny Fox Press LLC
5020 Kingsley Road
North Port, FL 34287

www.tinyfoxpress.com

CPSIA information can be obtained
at www.ICGtesting.com
Printed in the USA
LVHW110342220420
654204LV00002B/251